outside PERMISSION

Also by Eleanor Nilsson

FOR OLDER READERS
The House Guest

FOR MIDDLE READERS
The 89th Kitten
A Lamb Like Alice

FOR YOUNGER READERS
Pearl's Pantry
Heffalump?
Heffalump? and the Toy Hospital
The Black Duck
Pomily's Wish

PICTURE BOOKS
Parrot Fashion
The Rainbow Stealer
Tatty
A Bush Birthday
Mystery Meals
There's a Crocodile There Now Too

NON-FICTION
Writing for Children

outside
PERMISSION

Eleanor NILSSON

VIKING

Viking
Penguin Books Australia Ltd
487 Maroondah Highway, PO Box 257
Ringwood, Victoria 3134, Australia
Penguin Books Ltd
Harmondsworth, Middlesex, England
Viking Penguin, A Division of Penguin Books USA Inc.
375 Hudson Street, New York, New York 10014, USA
Penguin Books Canada Limited
10 Alcorn Avenue, Toronto, Ontario, Canada M4V 3B2
Penguin Books (N.Z.) Ltd
182-190 Wairau Road, Auckland 10, New Zealand

First published by Penguin Books Australia, 1996

1 3 5 7 9 10 8 6 4 2

Typeset in 10.5/14 Caslon 540 Roman by Post Typesetters
Printed and bound in Australia by Australian Print Group,
Maryborough, Vic.

National Library of Australia
Cataloguing-in-Publication data
Nilsson, Eleanor, 1939– .
Outside permission.
ISBN 0 670 86380 7.
I. Title.
A823.3

For Martin

I wish to express my sincere gratitude to the Literature Board of the Australia Council whose kind assistance enabled me to complete this book.

E.N.

Where the green swell is in the havens dumb,
And out of the swing of the sea.

Gerard Manley Hopkins

part **ONE**

'What about Simon?'

'Simon?'

'Yes.'

'Hatherley? You don't mean Simon Hatherley?'

'Yes.'

'Oh no. Not Simon.'

'Why not?'

'Because . . . Well, because . . . he's got everything. Looks, ability, friends. Now, even wealth. And nice with it. Everything.'

'Exactly.'

'What?'

'That's exactly what I mean.'

'But . . .'

'Yes. Simon. Simon Hatherley. Simon will do very well.'

chapter 1

DAVID AND SUSIE watched the Princes' team come out – with pride. They were both trying not to smile, but they knew their mouths were quirking up at the corners. They'd been so looking forward to it, this preliminary football match towards the end of summer. At first, when they'd watched the games, it had only been Simon they were interested in, but now they looked out for others in the team as well. Each player had his own way of moving, of handling the ball. After a while, you could pick up who was who and *that* was rewarding. Not by whether they were fair or dark, long-haired or short, chunky or spare, although that must, of course, come into it, but by how they handled the ball.

'There's Wright,' said Susie knowledgeably, 'back after a knee injury. That's a relief.'

Wright was their classy ruckman, not only winning most of the hit-outs, but a marvellous mark and a team player as well. He even shuffled around, folding himself up, to pick up balls coming out of the pack.

The team had finished jogging round the oval and were splitting off into their positions. It was easy to pick out Simon. His bright hair shone in the sun. Susie and David waited for him to line up either at centre or centre half-forward, his usual positions; but he jogged past centre, and was still jogging at the half-forward line.

'Must be going into the pocket,' said David.

'Or full forward.' Susie knew the coach had wanted to try him there before, but he'd resisted. Said he'd feel boxed in. Didn't want to just stand there leading and marking in a cage.

But it was to be full forward today. There he stood, blond, tall, right in front of goal. Hatherley. One season a new coach had decided to call them by their Christian names till he found out, according to Simon, that half of the players were called 'Matthew' and the other half 'Ben'.

5

Full forward. 'Whew!' said Susie, knowing what a responsibility it would be, especially today when they were playing the top team. 'This'll be something to watch. Poor Simon!'

David could feel excitement, elation, and nerves as the siren went and the umpire moved in for the centre bounce. He always felt like this, every time. He couldn't imagine what it must be like to be one of the players. You could feel a sense of bustle pass over the ground, then silence, as players and spectators and linesmen tuned in.

The knock to Wright, picked up by rover Marchant, marked by Dennig at half-forward. A punt kick into the fifty metre zone and here came the lead from Simon, and a beautiful sideways mark. 'Great play all the way down,' said Susie. 'Now kick it, Simon!'

Simon moved back, took his time, squared up his shoulders in line with the goals. He was on a slight angle, forty-five metres out. Far, but not too far. Not too far for Simon. Everything went quiet. The first goal often set the tone for the whole match. Here it came, straight as a die, right through the middle! Cheers and clapping. The coach, on the bench beside them, leaning forward in a concentrated way.

The ball at the centre bounce. The other way, this time. Almost a repeat performance, but in the wrong direction. The opposition's forward-pocket player lining up for goal, pulling up his socks, taking his time. Susie could feel her stomach tightening. Here it came. He'd missed! Only a point. Susie tried not to be over pleased. It had been a good bit of play too. She remembered her father saying that in his time you clapped good play, whichever side it was on.

Princes' full back kicking in, going up the side of the ground. Up to the half-back flank then marked at centre by Wright again. A long driving punt finding Archer who handpassed back to Marchant. One bounce, two; now the kick into the forward lines. A long lead out by Simon. 'He's marked it!' said Susie. 'Thirty metres in front!'

Again Simon taking his time, moving back slowly, lining up the ball. His long swinging stride forward, and the ball sailing between the posts. 'Two to Simon!' said Susie happily. 'This is going to be great.'

And it was. By half-time Princes were well ahead, four of the goals kicked by Simon. 10–6 to 3–8. 'A bit less than seven goals,' said Susie, grinning, 'but a handy lead.'

But after half-time the game grew messy, scrambly. And a strong wind gusted over the ground. Princes, kicking towards the northern end, into the teeth of the wind, found it was getting harder and harder to score. Meanwhile, at the other end, Rostrevor found they had the advantage of a three- or four-goal breeze. The wind was taking the ball, almost from centre it seemed, and carrying it between the big sticks. By three-quarter time, the difference was unaccountably only two points, with Princes just holding onto the lead.

Susie could see that Simon was chafing at having to stay in the goal square, was dying to have a run on the ball. But he was still there after the players broke from their huddle with the coach and set themselves for the last quarter. The wind, also unaccountably, had dropped, had become the gentlest of breezes.

Rostrevor got three goals in the first five minutes. Susie felt her heart sink. Wright had lost his dominance in the ruck, was maybe even limping a bit, and the whole side looked beat. Then the coach shifted Simon to centre.

Suddenly, Simon was everywhere. He was in the back lines, rescuing the ball, he was up forward scoring goals and sending brilliant handpasses to Marchant and Dennig, who were booting them in. Two more goals to Simon. One each to Marchant and Dennig. Eight points the difference. But then Rostrevor rallied, got a bag of three by cutting through on a wing and forward pocket. Princes had scored only one point. Nine points the difference, but the wrong way. Frantically, Susie consulted her watch. They couldn't be going to lose it now! And they must be in the time-on period. She could see the Princes' coach was having trouble keeping still. She couldn't herself. She jogged up and

7

down on the spot until David put a hand on each of her shoulders, pinning her down.

The centre bounce. Wright won it this time, punching the ball twenty metres, into the half-forward line. Picked up by their new rover – Susie didn't know his name, then to Marchant, but he'd run into a heap of players. There'd be a bounce, and time was running out. But here came a player breaking out of the pack with it: Simon! Sprinting up towards the goal, steadying himself, shooting at such an angle. A goal, a big one. Three points the difference. The whole thing was excruciating. Susie longed for it to be over, yet, at the same time, she wished it could go on for ever.

'Centre bounce will be crucial,' said David lugubriously, imitating the commentators they heard on the radio and TV.

But no, they'd lost it. Wright had overshot it somehow, and a Rostrevor player was banging the ball down into their forward lines. Here came Simon again, in the back lines now, racing out of nowhere and intercepting the pass. Booting it straight up the ground in the direction of Marchant and Glebe. No time to do anything else. Then running on, level with Marchant who'd marked. A handpass over and Simon with the ball again, running towards goal. Then, 'Oh no,' cried Susie, as he stumbled. 'Tripped,' said David, but the umpire hadn't seen it. Even as he fell, Simon managed to push the ball over to McKinnon, who ran into the open goal. Three points the difference; three points in front! Susie looked at her watch, longing for the siren. However much she willed it, it wouldn't go. They'd won the centre bounce, but a Rostrevor player had scrambled the ball out of the pack and booted it up to the half-forward line. Surely it must be time now. The half-forward, instead of kicking in to goal, had gone for a handpass. And there was Simon again, intercepting, throwing himself on the ball. The siren went as Simon scrambled to his feet.

The tired Princes' players shook hands with their opponents, then hugged one another in an ecstasy of goodwill and companionship. Their coach permitted himself a smile. A sweep of wind and rain blew across the ground, scattering the players and spectators like leaves.

chapter 2

THE NEXT DAY Susie and David hung around at home, waiting for Simon to turn up. They were still buoyed up from the afternoon before, longing to discuss the details of the match with him.

'That's odd,' said Susie. 'He nearly always comes over on Sundays, especially when he's played well!'

But it was a couple of weeks before he showed up – so unusual for Simon. He seemed restless, even irritable, and then nearly bit Susie's head off when she mentioned the game.

'You were great,' she said, following the boys up the stairs. 'Unstoppable in that last quarter.'

'Bloody invincible, was I?' He threw himself into David's easy chair.

Susie stared at him, but took the hint. 'I think I'll go wash my hair,' she said, wandering off.

'Good,' said Simon, as the last of her disappeared. 'I've been wanting to ask you something.' He glanced around David's attic room as if what he was to ask were hidden in its pine walls. Then he got up and sprawled across David's oak chest. 'They say . . . some people know.'

'Know what?' asked David, as he was meant to. It irritated him the way Simon often spoke in puzzles, just to tease the questions out of him.

'You know. *Know*.' (He underlined the word heavily with his voice.)

'No, I don't know. Otherwise I wouldn't be asking, would I?'

'Know about themselves. Know about the future. Seen *The Book of Records.*'

'Bully for them' said David, at the same time feeling his stomach lurch, then turn over.

'Wouldn't you?'

'What?'

'Want to know.'

'Hardly.'

'Why?'

'It's better not to. Spoils all the fun, what there is of it. Some things you're better off not knowing.'

'I dare you,' said Simon.

'Dare me what?'

'To find out.'

'No way.' David tossed his thick dark hair back as he did when he was worried. That was asking too much. That was going far too far. 'Dare yourself.'

'I might just do that.' Then, quietly, 'Chicken.'

David was surprised; even upset. It wasn't like Simon to speak like that. Not that he'd ever given him much opportunity before. They'd always played at dares and challenges, right from primary school. A dare was different from a challenge. A challenge might be jumping in at the deep end of the pool, or later, diving in. Later still, swimming a mile without stopping. But a dare had a darker sort of edge to it. Something forbidden. Like diving out of the back window of the classroom when nobody was looking. Giving a teacher the wrong message. More recently, pretending they were staying at each other's house when they were really doing something quite other. Once they had both lived in the same street, opposite the Unley pool. Then Simon's dad had made a fortune out of computers, and they'd bought a house off Victoria Drive. Now Simon went to a private school, but they had still stayed friends. And the dares went on. But there had never been a dare like this. Not just forbidden. Unthinkable. Taboo.

'Wait on. It's not that I'm chicken.' There was a tight feeling in

David's chest. 'It's just, I can't see the point. Why mess around? Why mess around with . . . ?'

But Simon's face was already closing over. He turned away from David, then suddenly levered himself up off the old oak chest, bent his head under the lintel and belted down the attic stairs far faster than was safe.

David looked around at his room, its peace shattered, his contentment spoiled. He'd been looking forward to a really happy weekend. Talk about an over-reaction. And Simon had even sworn at Susie, or in her direction. Yet a couple of times lately he'd caught him looking at her that way. Not just friendly, more calculating. A 'what would it be like to . . . ?' kind of a look.

'Where's Simon off to in such a hurry?' It was his mother, emerging from her room with someone's manuscript tucked, as usual, under her arm. 'One day he'll kill himself on those stairs. I was hoping you'd both have a read of this.'

David groaned. He was coming down the stairs himself, heading for the fridge. Something to eat might settle him down. He was glad they'd had the attic room fitted out for him when he'd started high school. It was the only way you could get any sort of privacy in their house.

It was a single-fronted bluestone 'villa' as it would say in a real estate ad, with a narrow drive running down one side. Yet the house and its block were deceptively deep. Rooms ran in a row like carriages in the trains that rattled past all day. On summer nights his mum, in the middle of editing a manuscript, couldn't stand it any more. Happy screams would be coming from the pool; freight trains plodding past. The noises would be accentuated by the heat and by the stuffiness inside. She'd turn up the radio so high, to shut it all out with a noise of her own choosing, that he'd have to hide in the attic or run from the house.

Susie came through to the kitchen with her hair in a towel. 'Mum, can I go out with Cynth tonight?'

'No.'

'Just to the Capri and straight home.'

'No.'

'Why?'

'You're too young and Cynthia looks too grown-up.'

'She does,' said Susie, agreeing sensibly, 'but she acts grown-up too. What if Dave comes with us?'

'I've seen that film,' he said, without thinking. (Most things he would do for Susie.) 'Why not just pick up a video?'

'That's a good idea.' Their mother was obviously relieved. 'Ring Cynthia up and ask her for tea. I'll make vegetarian lasagne for her. Or moussaka, without the mince.'

'Oh, Mum.'

'What's wrong now?'

'It's not like going out. Not like an outing.'

'You can have plenty of outings during the day.'

The video had been a lot about water, David thought; water with dramatic music over it. It would have seemed more disturbing, perhaps, if most of the shots hadn't been taken at night, so that everything became indistinct, even if vaguely scary. Although water – grey, amorphous, indistinct water – could be very scary, and was associated in his mind with an undefined fear he had about suffocation. Yet he loved the beach, the sea. He loved it almost as much as Simon did.

He'd taken the most comfortable chair, dozed off in it. He woke to hear the girls' voices coming as if from far away. The movie must be finished then, or they'd got bored with it as well.

'I think Simon's terrific-looking,' Susie was saying. 'I really like blond hair with brown eyes. Unusual. But it doesn't have any effect on me. He's almost too good-looking, like a painting that you stare at but can't really relate to. I wouldn't want to go out with him.'

Cynthia sighed. 'You go out with him all the time.'

'Yes, but not in that way. We just all hang out together. I'd never want specially to be alone with him, but then, I wouldn't mind either. He just doesn't have any effect on me.'

12

'You'd be on your own, then. Maybe it's because you've known him so long. He's much better looking than David.'

'Maybe. But I like the way Dave looks, better. Craggy. Sort of dependable. And I like dark brown hair. Like liquorice, but shiny. When you really look at Simon, his eyes are a bit small. He looks wary.'

David smirked to himself, pleased that Susie had absolutely no interest in Simon. Or not in that way. He didn't want things to get complicated. He wanted them, he thought, with a sudden anxious feeling that everything might be about to slide away, he wanted them to stay essentially the same. He hoped, especially, that Simon would forget all about his latest senseless, ridiculous, outrageous dare.

chapter 3

BUT THE NEXT time they met, on Wednesday, it was clear Simon hadn't forgotten. He was quite cool, in the sense of chilly, and he hadn't come round to see David as he usually did early in the week. David had had to seek him out at the big house that he didn't feel really comfortable in. It seemed funny, seeing the same people, but in so different a setting. No lopsided, strange little attic rooms here. A whole extra storey, with pale carpets everywhere, and antique pieces gradually edging out the homely furniture he had loved. David didn't think much usually about how adults felt, but he'd noticed Simon's mum didn't seem as happy as he would have expected in the new house. She might feel uneasy in it, as he did.

'Hi, David,' she said, her face lighting up. That was one thing he really liked about her. She was always so genuinely pleased to see him. 'Haven't seen you for ages. How's things? School work okay?'

'Fine.' Just a million projects he should have been getting stuck into and couldn't, because of Simon's stupid dare.

He sat down uneasily on a velvet couch. He thought of the sofa in their old house, friendly and stained, with the stuffing falling out underneath. This lounge had a breathless quality about it: as if you had to hold your breath, talk in whispers when you were in it. He looked out at the view, framed in a bay window, with bench seats tucked neatly underneath it. His mother would kill for a room like this. He searched desperately through his mind for something sensible that he might be able to talk to her about. 'You know the shop at the end of our street. They've painted it the most sickening yellow colour. It's so bright, people nearly fall out of their cars looking at it.'

'*Have* they? You mean the tile place that looks like a castle? How odd. Still, maybe it does mean people'll notice it. Shopkeepers will try anything in a recession, won't they?'

David nodded, feeling uneasy again at the mention of anything to do with money, for talk of it reminded him of the difference between the two families, between the then and the now. He was glad when Simon appeared, leaning into the doorway, even if he was strained-looking, unsmiling.

'Come for a ride?' David asked, half expecting him to say no. But Simon had nodded and come.

They bumped down King William Road, over the bricks, then through to the parklands, in almost complete silence. When David couldn't stand it any longer, he brought his bicycle to a halt. 'Look, what's all the sweat? Why don't we wait till next year? A building that size, what hope would we have?' He didn't name it. Even the thought of the building, let alone the name of it, made him shudder. 'And we've got our exams. A delayed dare. What d'you say?'

It wasn't like Simon to sulk around like this. Still, a dare had always been a dare. If Simon insisted, he'd have to do it.

'Why not make it ten years? Twenty? What sort of dare is that? A dare in the future. I want to do it now.'

'You mean in a few weeks?'

Simon looked as if he would explode – or implode. His voice was shaking. 'I mean, *now*. This week. This Saturday.'

David gasped. He felt his palms run, suddenly, with sweat.

'What's so urgent?'

'I just want-to-do-it-*now*.'

David could understand that too. He knew what it was like to want something, and to want it right away. Only, it seemed such a bizarre, possibly catastrophic thing to want. To see into *The Book of Records*. Or would they be files? And why on earth should Simon want it? And why now? Yet he found himself agreeing. 'Okay,' he said. And felt instantly flooded with dismay.

Straight away, Simon changed back to his usual self. He slapped him on the shoulder. 'Thanks, Dave. I knew you'd do it.' His voice was excited. 'Now, we'll go on Saturday and suss the place out. They're open on Saturdays now. Not try anything, just have a look around.'

David pretended to be studying the Adelaide rosellas hanging upside down in the gum tree next to them. If you looked in among the leaves you could see the white blossoms they were probably after. 'Okay,' he said again, after a long pause. Surely it would be impossible anyway. They'd never be allowed to get near.

David spent an awful couple of days: nearly crashing his mum's car, forgetting to hand in a maths assignment, forgetting to *do* an English one. He even fell over the mat trying to get into the house, and grazed his head on the doorframe. 'Growing too fast,' said his mum. 'Getting clumsy. Wish it was me. Growing, I mean.'

By Saturday morning he felt sullen, leaden, aggrieved. Out of his window the sky looked blue, the day golden. He almost wished for rain. What if they got caught, snooping around? What would happen then? He was meeting Simon in town, at the bus stop in front of Parliament House.

He dressed slowly, trying to remember what he knew about The House of Records. But his mind baulked at it, wanted to think of other things. He half hoped he'd miss the train, but caught it with a couple of minutes to spare and sat looking drearily out through a smeary window at run-down backyards and then at a crowded cemetery. Maybe Simon wouldn't be there; but even in the distance he could see him, his blond hair sitting on his head like a thatch.

Today, Simon seemed almost too bright. 'You look like you're going to a funeral,' he said breezily, pushing David onto the bus. He pulled a strange little navy cap from his pocket and put it on. 'Cheer up. You might even enjoy it.'

David doubted it. He doubted it even more when out of a flat industrial landscape The House of Records came into view. It was a heavy, grey, austere-looking building set up on a slight hill with tiers of curving grey, heavy steps leading up to it. Funereal. David remembered being there with his mother once or twice as a child, to pick up birth certificates perhaps, and was surprised to find that the place appeared the same, gave him the same shuddery feeling as it had then. It hadn't shrunk, dwindled, as places often did as you grew older.

The bus whined to a stop. David got off almost first. Grit blew up in his face. He remembered how an unpleasant wind always seemed to blow around here. The few trees in the car park looked grey and discouraged and were bent into odd shapes. He remembered too how the staff here were all dressed like old-fashioned tailors' dummies, hardly alive, in dark grey suits, stiff white shirts and subdued ties. The rooms were painted off-white, the desks black, so that the only colour in the building came from the screens of the computers. Perhaps from the carpets as well; he wasn't sure.

He and Simon had dressed up (or down) for the occasion, in the most inconspicuous garb they could think of: dark navy trousers (not jeans), white shirts, navy pullovers (not skivvies). They looked quiet and respectable, almost like recruits for The House of Records itself. They walked steadily through the grey halls – grey marbled flooring, and yes, colour at last. Dark red runners ran down the centre of them. Glassed-off rooms lay on either side.

Their plan was to keep walking until someone should challenge them. It happened at the end of the first hall.

'Can I help you?' asked a grey-faced official, coming round the door of his glassed-in office, bundles of paper under his arm.

'No,' David said quickly. 'We have an appointment.' He pointed upwards, then glanced at his watch.

And, walking as confidently as they could, they rounded the corner and headed up the stairs.

The second floor was an office floor, and much like the first. Everyone seemed too busy to notice them and they reached the next lot of stairs without any trouble.

'If we knew what we were looking *for* it would be a lot easier,' whispered Simon. 'High-security information like this isn't likely to be on the lower floors. Why don't we start at the top down?'

'Okay,' said David, talking in a normal voice which he felt would attract less attention. 'But let's use the stairs.' They might be too conspicuous in the lifts, two boys on their own, although they'd been wise to choose the lunch hour when there was a lot of coming and going from incomers as well as from staff. The subdued atmosphere of the building seemed to affect everyone, so that on the third floor, clearly a public floor, everywhere there were whispery groups waiting in queues.

They went up and up the spiralling stairs which had the same curve to them as David had noticed on the steps outside. Fourth floor, fifth. All public. David noticed that Simon was breathing heavily – panting almost, his mouth open. 'Boy, what's happened to you? Anyone'd think you're unfit! What's the coach going to say when you front up for training next week?'

'I'll pick up swimming again soon.' Simon gasped. 'And gym.' His face was pale, his forehead beaded in sweat. 'Stairs always get me down.'

'And sometimes up.'

'Ha, ha. But I'm thinking of giving footy a miss this year.'

David stared at him. 'But you're crazy about football. Susie'd kill you.'

'I know, but with exams. It takes up a lot of time. I sort of promised Mum. I sure will miss it, though,' he added, half to himself.

Sixth, seventh, eighth. Simon had slowed almost to a standstill.

'Look,' said David, 'you take the lift. I'll stick to the stairs – that'll give us a double chance. If we miss each other, let's find our own way home. I don't like the idea of hanging around outside.'

Simon nodded, almost as if he couldn't talk, and David bounded up the stairs on his own. It wasn't often he could outlast Simon like this. He'd probably had too much breakfast, or else was feeling even more jittery than David was. And Simon, giving up on football! That was really weird.

He realised that rushing it had been a stupid thing to do when he nearly collided with an official – sober, compact and carrying a dark briefcase. He could feel the equally dark eyes following him as he walked more sedately round the next curve. Now there were small arrow-slit windows on the straight edge of the stairs, just before the sharp curve up. He'd been sure the windows had been ordinary oblongs lower down, or he'd have noticed. He rose on tiptoe and looked out of one of them. It might calm his nerves to look out over the city. But somehow it didn't. The buildings seemed distorted, as if the glass in the window wasn't quite true. He shook his head and climbed higher, up and up, till his chest grew tight.

He'd decided to stop on the second to highest floor. It would be foolish to go further. If the top floor held the crucial records, there would be restricted access. You couldn't just barge out onto it with some inane excuse or other. There might even be security guards up here with guns. Knowledge like this could ruin the health service, spark off riots, cause people to act out of character. Make society, as they knew it, impossible. He was mad to have come.

Feeling shaky, he walked out onto what should be the floor he wanted. '30' said the sign. He caught only a glimpse, when suddenly the space behind him filled in, and a hand was on his shoulder, turning him around.

'May I help you?' The words were polite but the tone wasn't. David fixed his eyes on a grey-on-grey striped tie sitting perfectly knotted over a crisp white shirt.

'I'm meeting my mum here,' he said. 'Need a copy of my birth certificate. "Floor 30", she said.'

The hand relaxed on his shoulder. '*Thirteen* is what you want.'

'What?' David turned his head to the side.

The official raised his voice. '*Thirteen*. The public are not allowed access beyond the lower floors.'

('He spoke just like a dummy,' he said to Simon later.

'Dummies don't speak.')

The official steered him carefully into the lift, conveniently waiting, and followed him in. David got the feeling from the pressure in his back that he would have propelled him into the space even if the lift hadn't been there.

It slid smoothly down. David longed for it to stop, to fill up with people, to become normal. He stared at the panel to avoid looking up at the man. *Basement, Ground, 1, 2, 3, 17, 18, 26, 27* ... His eyes moved up lazily, then focused sharply. That was odd. That was *very* odd. He must remember to tell Simon. It might be their first clue.

The doors opened at Floor 19 and several people hurried in. David flattened himself against the side and towards the front so that he could rush out as soon as the door opened. He looked around for the official. He appeared quite relaxed, his head almost touching the roof, his blue eyes looking out beyond David. But David knew that sort of look. It was the look his English teacher often used. He'd fix his eyes on the middle distance but you knew he was really looking sideways at you.

The lift stopped at Floor 13. David waited politely for the lady with the pusher to get out first. He strode out slowly, his shoulders squared, his heart thumping. He knew he was being watched and that he mustn't run.

19

It was a busy floor, with long queues waiting at each tired counter. He walked slowly from line to line. If only he knew someone, he could pretend they were his mother. He joined a queue. He waited and waited. He would ask if he could get a copy himself, or if his mother had already picked one up. His legs were aching and sore. Surely the blue-eyed official would have given up by now? He looked at the clock, placed centrally on the high white wall. A round window with segmented panes lay above it. He couldn't stay here for ever. But, as he jerked himself around, boiling with frustration, ready to head off, he had a sudden crawly feeling up his spine as if he were being watched. It was just nerves, of course. He stood still for a minute or two, then turned around more slowly. And there, over by the clock wall, and certainly watching him, stood the official he'd met on the stairs.

chapter 4

WHEN DAVID MANAGED to catch hold of Simon, Simon had been evasive. And 'catch' had been the word. He'd gone round on Sunday.

'Oh. David. How are you?' his mother asked in a perfunctory way, her face not lighting up, not pleased to see him. And she hadn't invited him in. 'Simon's gone out. He'll be out all day.'

And that was it. He'd felt really hurt. It wasn't just Simon who was acting weird. Only Ged, the elderly black labrador, had given him any sort of welcome at all.

But he wasn't going to be put off. He cycled back on Monday as soon as he knew Simon would have got home from school. This time it was Simon who came to the door. He led him out to the front garden, away from the house. David put his arm around one

of the thick trunks of red gum. Simon stood dourly, listless, looking down.

'Well, what happened?'

'Happened?' Simon was ridiculously, ludicrously vague.

'When you went up in the lift.'

'Oh, nothing much. When the last people were getting out at
one of the floors I thought I'd better too.'

'Why? If there was no one there.'

'There was an official in the lift. He was looking at me in a
funny way.'

'And didn't you go up the steps then?'

'I didn't feel . . . No, I just had to get out.'

'Had to?'

'I mean, it all seemed a bit useless.'

'*Useless?*' So much for the important quest; the quest that
couldn't wait. And it had been quite interesting in its way, the
visit to The House of Records. He could think that, now he was
out of it. David dug his toe angrily into the perfect lawn and rode
off, because it didn't look as if even Simon were going to invite
him in. What he'd feared, was beginning to happen. The wealth,
the private school, the living off Victoria Drive, was going to the
Hatherleys' heads. Never mind: he had other friends. But he
knew he didn't, really. Not friends like Simon. Andrew and Tim
and Nick were only a group he'd hung around with since Simon
had left.

He spent the next day feeling miserable, but when Simon had
come round on Wednesday, and belted up the stairs to David's
room, he'd seemed quite different. Enthusiastic. Intense. Wanting all the details of what David had done. At first he'd felt
irritated, but when he saw that Simon was genuinely interested,
interested especially in the strange numbering on the lift, he got
excited about it again himself.

'The floor I'd got up to said "30". I'm sure it did. On a wooden
board at the front just before the computers started. But the top
floor listed in the lift was 28. I just got a glimpse, but . . . No, it

21

must have been "30", because when I said I'd been looking for births, he seemed relieved. Said it was "13", which could have been an honest mistake, I suppose. And I pretended to be a bit deaf.' It had been one of their more irritating ploys in primary school to prevent teachers from cross-examining them. 'He spoke like a recorded message. Part human.' He paused, looking for a response.

'Scary.'

David nodded. 'He said something about the public not being allowed beyond the bottom floors. That seemed a weird way to put it. Why not "beyond floor 20", say?'

'Because they don't want you to know which floors are important.'

'Even if we pick the right floor, how're we going to see the health files?'

'I guess they're just people like anybody else,' said Simon. 'Even if they seem in training for robots. People get careless or tired or inattentive. There has to be a way. Anyway, I reckon you've found the right floor. It's there, or thereabouts.'

David thought about the long room, the room he'd only got a glimpse of: the wall of glass, the network of computers, the green strip of carpet. There had been something strange about the room, or about the feeling that it gave him. He tried to visualise it again. No, seemed okay. Yet his stomach went into knots as he pictured it.

'Let's raid the fridge.' But he hastily backed into the attic again when he saw his mother roaming around the house with a teetering pile of manuscripts. At least he could protect Simon from having to read the stuff.

'Can I come up here for a bit?' Susie's voice was querulous. She tiptoed up the stairs. 'I'd just like to read a proper published book in peace.'

'At least your mum *does* something,' said Simon. 'Mine just cooks and reads the paper. Goes for walks. Sings in the choir.'

'Sounds all right to me.'

'No, it's not, really. She always wanted to be a nurse, but now she says if she finishes her training it's taking jobs away from people like us.'

'I don't want to be a nurse,' said David. 'Not even a male one.'

'No, but you know what I mean. Her life will be pointless when I'm . . . not there.'

'What a funny way to put it!' said Susie.

'Funny?'

'Yes. I thought you'd say, "when I leave home", or something. Just seemed odd. Sorry. But then everything does seem odd after I've been reading Mum's stories.'

'Susie! Susie! Where are you?'

'I'm off. I'm definitely off this time. I'm going for a swim with my book.'

'Poor book,' said Simon. 'That shows you're really off. Bye. But we might follow you in a tick.' He turned to David. 'Remember that American book your mum read to us when we were small? About two kids who camped out in the Metropolitan Art Museum?'

'Vaguely. Why?'

'D'you remember how they fixed it so they could stay in there at night?'

David looked at him. He did remember that part. His heart sank. 'You don't mean . . . ?'

'I do mean. That's exactly what I mean.'

It was 5.12 on Friday night when they drove through the car park at The House of Records. Simon wanted to leave the car in a street behind it. He chose to drive through the coloured cars at one end. It looked friendlier, somehow. It was only when they walked back they realised the other end was for officials' cars only. 'That explains it,' said Simon. 'Like we said before. "Dummies". "Robots". They all drive white cars.'

David looked at the immaculate rows, all the cars sitting very straight between cleanly marked white lines. There were some four-wheel drives among them. Even these were white. 'For safety,' he suggested.

'Or anonymity.'

'That's a big word.'

'It comes out of a big brain.'

The last buses were leaving. Only a few people were coming down the steps, and no one was going up them. David realised they'd made themselves look conspicuous by coming so late, not that they'd had much choice. He hovered at the bottom of the steps. But Simon was already bounding up them. The afternoon sun lit up his shining hair.

They'd only just got inside when alarm bells began to ring. The tone was harsh, grating. David jumped, looked around him guiltily, preparing to run. They must have been spotted.

'It'll only be to clear the building,' Simon whispered. 'Let's make ourselves scarce.'

They headed for the toilets near the entrance. David curled himself up on one toilet seat, Simon on the other. They left the doors slightly ajar. It was 5.25 p.m.

'Those guys – in the book – must've been a lot smaller than us,' whispered David.

'Don't talk.'

David listened to the last rush of customers and staff heading out the doors. Again, though, he got the sense of subdued conversation. Everything seemed muted inside this building. He looked around him. The toilet walls were tiled in grey, the doors black, washbasins white. All part of the cheerful, let's have fun, kind of image. The security guard should be around soon with his pistol. Or maybe they had rifles here. He felt bloody stupid sitting curled up on the seat. Only pre-electronic kids could hide like this and get away with it. Anyway, he thought uncomfortably, it had only been in a story. That didn't prove it would really have worked. The chocolate bars he'd brought jabbed him uncomfortably in the ribs. And he'd nearly lost one banana already, as his sock spiralled downwards.

24

When they got down and tried to walk across the floor, alarm bells were sure to go off all over the building. What would the punishment be? He pictured their heads sticking out of the turrets of the old Adelaide prison, restored especially for them, or else out north, dressed in another kind of uniform, at that dreary high-security prison on the main road. He thought longingly of home, even with those awful manuscripts. It was at that moment, high up on a wall, grey on grey, he saw it: a camera, staring down at him out of a blank eye.

chapter 5

AGES LATER, SIMON decided it was safe to get down and stumble out to the corridor.

'This has been such a dumb idea,' said David, rubbing at his stiff legs. 'There was a camera in that washroom. There'll be cameras all over the place.'

'Of course. What did you expect? But they're turned off.'

'Turned *off*?'

'I'll explain later. Just follow me – and don't talk.'

The building lay in eerie quiet, natural light still streaming brightly in through windows set high up in the walls. But the light had a pink glow to it: soon it would be dark. The ground floor looked as it had before, without the subdued noise, without the people. It had the hush of a church – or of a mortuary. That was more like it. As if the officials were all stretched out stiff in their cubicles, where they might (perhaps) revive in the morning.

They climbed the stairs carefully, high-stepping to deaden the noise, hugging the wall as the light slowly faded. By the time they reached the arrow-slit windows on the floors higher up, stars were brightening out of a dulling sky. Why do I end up back here? thought David. And what did Simon mean about the cameras? He was treating him like a kid. So far, it was much too easy.

Almost dark now and Simon, half a curve ahead of him, had become just a shape. Then, as he turned a corner, the stairs were bathed in blinding light. He froze.

'It's okay,' Simon whispered, tiptoeing down the stairs towards him. 'It's the security lights. Selected lights in the building will be going on now.'

How does he know? thought David. How does he know all this stuff? Or is he guessing?

At each stairhead, Simon checked the floor numbers. It was as David had told him: the numbers were marked on wooden boards at the end of each floor. 23, 24, 25. Every floor was marked in sequence, perfectly normally. 26, 27 . . . The numbers blurred as David looked at them. Simon seemed to be taking this visit much more in his stride than he was. The thought annoyed him.

28 on the wooden board, the long room behind it, lying bathed in white light. Too bright, fluorescent – unreal light. Floor 28, the last floor marked on the lift. He looked beyond it, up the stair-well. The taste of chocolate and banana, mixed uneasily together, was in his mouth. He swallowed hastily. The stairwell was in darkness. There were no lights above the twenty-eighth floor. He thought with a sudden ache of Susie, peacefully watching televi-sion, curled up on the old brown sofa. She'd be thinking *he* was the lucky one. Floor 29 in darkness. David tried not to think of food. They'd never get further than this. His feet searched for trip cords on every step. Cords that would trigger alarms. But nothing went off; nothing happened.

And then, on a lower floor, he heard a door bang, footsteps and the steady hum of the lift. Simon stood stiff beside him, rigid with tension. David moved further up the stairway and glimpsed stars out of an arrow-slit window. Stars usually made him feel he was exaggerating.

'The lift's gone down again,' hissed Simon. 'We're in luck!'

Round the curve and up to Floor 30. He'd been wrong that first time. He *had* come out on the highest floor. The stairs petered out, just past it. So it had to be this floor or the one below it: the two floors that didn't exist on the lift directory, the two floors that were hidden in darkness. Except that Floor 30 wasn't. A subdued light shone over one desk: an official busy with his computer, a print-out flowing steadily into his work tray at the side.

They sank back into the darkness of the stair. David felt relieved and disappointed at the same time. This was probably the place, these were probably the files, but their chances of seeing them were still exactly zero. They crept back to Floor 29.

'That's it, then,' said David.

Simon wasn't listening. He was peering up the stairwell again. He came back to David. 'You stay here and have a look around. I'll wait upstairs. See if he goes to the toilet or something.'

'That wouldn't give you long. Anyway, it's too . . .'

But Simon was off. David forced himself to investigate. He took out his small torch. Floor 29 seemed much like Floor 30, as he remembered it, except that there were more filing cabinets and rather less computers.

Systematically he tried the filing cabinets along one wall and up the other. They were numbered 1 to 52, with no other sign of identification, and were all, convincingly, locked. Perhaps they were birth records, he thought, feeling clever. One cabinet for each week of the year. Equally, of course, they could be records of death.

What was that? He held himself still, then slipped in quickly behind a filing cabinet. The metal felt cold against his body. He listened. There it was again: a faint, muffled sound. But it was only Simon.

'He's updating the files, for sure. Seems odd he's alone – but that must be the reason. Security, I mean. If you'd make a noise down here . . .' He looked around him. 'Give me time to get up the stairs again, then drop the wastepaper basket onto the desk. If that doesn't work, throw it against a window.'

'Where you going to hide?'

But Simon had already gone.

David waited; then, just as he went to pick up the basket, there it was again, that muffled sound on the stairs. It would be Simon, changing his mind about what they should do. He nearly called out to him, but slid behind a filing cabinet just in case. It was only then he realised the sound had been of coming *up* the stairs, and not down them. He crouched against the wall. Air shifted in the doorway. A torch was flashed quickly around, and immediately clicked off.

He kept as still as he could as the figure left Floor 29 and started to climb steadily up the last long flight of stairs. David thought of Simon, squeezed between the stairway and the room: not able to go inside to hide, not able to stay out. Even worse, he might think it was David. I should have tossed the basket at the window, to warn him, he thought. But it was too late. The footsteps had stopped. He waited for a raised voice at least; maybe even a shot. Nothing. Then he heard the same footsteps, the same feet, walking in a measured way down the stairs again.

'How'd you get out of that?' They were back in the toilets again, waiting for morning.

'I went and sat at the desk.'

'*What*?'

'The official had just left, to have a fag maybe. He'd gone out the other end. I heard the footsteps, too heavy for you. So, I sat at his desk.'

'In the light?'

'Seemed safest. Anyhow, the light was dim, shadowy, and I turned it sideways a bit. I kept my head down, just lifted my hand as a greeting. I didn't look up. Also I was hoping to find something out.'

David stared at Simon. Did he know him at all? 'You could be in a spy movie any time. Some cool customer! And did you?'

'What?'

28

'Find out anything.'

'No. Or only that it's the right spot. You'd think they'd be more subtle than that. Make it Floor 12, say, somewhere tucked in among the normal floors. He'd been updating the files. "Forward projections". But as soon as the security guard went away, I got out again. I couldn't very well wave at the official too, say I'd been keeping the seat warm, could I?'

'I reckon, on this dare, you could do just about anything.'

'And then, not long after that, he packed up and left. There was no chance to try again.' He sighed.

'Well, that's about it, isn't it?' said David, more comfortably. 'That's twice we tried. Honour is satisfied.'

'But curiosity isn't. We'll give it one more go. Three's lucky.'

'"Lucky" could be unlucky.' Were they never to be rid of this place? And why was Simon so keen? Fanatical, obsessed, might be closer to it. 'We can't just do the same old thing again.'

The washroom floor was cold and hard under him. He was wishing he'd brought a rug. Sleeping under the stars was much more pleasant (and hygienic) than this.

'It won't be the same thing again. Nothing ever is. Anyhow, we'll think of something different.'

David tried to put himself into a sleeping position. But his mind was racing. He lay on one arm, and turned to face the outer wall. There was a small door or cupboard set into it he hadn't really noticed before. He got up and searched for a way in. He pictured blankets, pillows, an offcut of carpet perhaps. He tugged on the door. It was sticking, but suddenly it flew open. The handle of a mop fell out and hit him. It was only a cleaning cupboard. He kicked the door shut and lay down. Impossible. He sat up again, took off his jumper and spread it under him. There, that was better. Lumpier, but not so cold. He'd never sleep, though. Simon was lying nearby, apparently contented, as if in his bed at home. But he must have dozed off, for when he opened his eyes he was lying on his back staring up at the camera, the first early light spilling in through the small round window beneath it.

29

chapter 6

'DID YOU HAVE a nice time at Simon's?'

David propped his head up wearily over the marmalade.

'David. At Simon's. Did you have a nice time?'

'Not bad.' He sighed at the effort of having to speak at all.

'I've been dying to hear more about the house. Did you notice this visit, are all the bedrooms upstairs?'

'Um. I think so. Yeah, I suppose they are.'

'It's a bit early for him yet,' said Susie. 'His memory'll get better later in the day.'

'I certainly hope so. You weren't drinking, were you, David?'

'No, Mum.'

'You and Simon aren't getting up to anything silly, are you?'

'No, Mum. No alcohol, no drugs, not even any girls.'

'And don't talk about girls like that. Always show proper respect.'

'Mum, give me a break, will you? I didn't sleep well, that's all.' He shoved the marmalade away. 'I'm off for a swim. Maybe it'll wake me up.'

The council pool opposite had always been a marvellous source of escape for David and Susie. When their father had lived at home and there had been dark silences over the house, the children had often vanished into the space and light of the blue water.

David plunged into the pool (really far too cold yet), and raced up and down to get warm. Then he pulled himself out and sat, to drip dry, on the grass. He felt revived but fragile. He kept thinking about The House of Records and about how brave Simon had been. Not just brave, enterprising. Reckless. David knew that if he didn't take the initiative soon, he'd just be trudging behind. He'd still have to do it, but in second place, without honour. They both knew they needed to do something different. But what? Maybe if somebody else came with them . . .

30

Susie appeared, swinging her towel. She bounced down beside him, and then up again, at once. 'Don't go away,' she said, and dived cleanly off the side.

David watched her. She was a beautiful swimmer, hardly disturbing the water, cutting through it like some superior kind of iridescent pink fish. David was good and Simon reasonable, but they lacked grace, and with it, Susie's efficiency. Maybe, too, it was because she'd started younger than they had. She'd had a slight heart defect when she'd been little, and her mum had rushed her off to the pool. 'Swimming's the thing,' their doctor had said. She had the right temperament too: never got rattled, never seemed nervy.

Susie swam steadily, length upon length. The pool was Olympic size but she made it seem smaller. They still had it all to themselves.

'Twenty laps. Not bad, straight after breakfast. Now, tell me what's going on.' She screwed up her face in delighted anticipation. 'What were you and Simon up to last night?'

'What d'you mean, "up to"?' He played for time; because he was so tired he might let something slip. He looked at her out of half-closed eyes, squinting against the sun.

'There's something going on. I can always tell.'

'You've a great imagination, kid. Nothing much goes on around here. We stayed up late, watched a video. Okay, two videos. Then a late movie . . .'

'That's not what I mean. I mean about you coming home. You're never back before lunchtime at least. Did you have a fight?'

'No,' he said. Then wished he hadn't. The thought of a quarrel would've kept her quiet. Now she still looked speculative.

'No, of course not,' she muttered, half to herself. 'You never fight with Simon.'

But she was wrong about that. She hovered at first, when Simon popped in the next day. He still looked short on sleep.

31

David's mother picked up on it. 'You looking after yourself, Simon? You seem to be getting taller and taller and thinner and thinner. You look peaky. Have a bit of streusel, fresh out the oven. Build yourself up.'

'Thanks.' Simon grinned, looked somehow relieved, and cut himself what he called a largish square. 'More of a giant oblong,' said Susie, cutting off a smaller piece for herself. 'Anyone feel like going down the beach? Greg (you know, Cynth's brother), he's taking us down.' She glanced at her watch. 'In about half an hour. I said you might come. At least I said Dave might, but they'd have room for both of you.'

'You'd have to sit on my knee,' said Simon, winking at her. 'But no, thanks. I haven't got my bathers . . .'

'Dave's got two pairs.'

'No,' said David. 'We don't feel like it today.'

'Stodgy pair,' said their mum.

But David and Simon were already drifting off to the attic room, carrying with them extra slices of still-steaming streusel.

Simon sat down on the oak chest. 'I thought we might try again next Saturday.'

He was getting straight to the point. The only point he seemed to see these days, David thought wryly, swinging himself into his easy chair. Really, when you thought about it, he was spending far more time on The House of Records thing than he ever would have on his footy.

Simon went on, 'Saturday might be better. You wouldn't be so likely to get people working back on a Saturday night.'

David considered it. 'But how would we get out? We might get stuck inside till Monday.'

Simon's usually easy-going face suddenly looked stubborn, even sulky.

'And if no one's working back, updating the files, how're you going to get at them? They're not likely to leave them lying around.'

'That's a point,' mumbled Simon. 'Maybe we should keep to Friday.'

'Now tell me about the cameras: how you know they're switched off.'

'Oh that.' Simon looked vague. 'This man at the . . .' He paused then started again. Susie had been right, Simon's eyes *did* look wary. 'This guy I met said they've got security cameras everywhere in the building. But they're just a blind. Or at least they're turned off. They found it was more dangerous having them on. If a film got stolen, someone outside would have a plan of the whole building, of where the files are.'

'How weird. Some waste of money. Although I suppose it would still work – if people *think* they're on, I mean.' He studied the knots in the pine boards on the nearest wall. 'Look, I've been thinking.'

David waited for the usual kind of response: 'Should you?'; 'Careful'; 'So that's what's wrong'; 'Have you checked with your doctor?' But it didn't come. Simon simply looked attentively, even hopefully, at him.

'We can't keep doing the same thing. We've gotta have something new.'

'What sort of something?'

'Some sort of distraction. You know how in films, or even in mum's manuscripts, if someone wants to do something, they provide a diversion, don't they? So everyone's looking one way, but the real action . . .'

'Is somewhere else. Like you were going to do the other night.'

'Maybe we need someone else with us.'

'There's no one else we could trust. Except, of course . . .'

'*No*,' said David. 'You can leave Susie out of this.'

'Okay, okay. Anyway, that's what I said to this guy.'

'What guy?'

'The guy that told me about the cameras.' Simon spoke slowly as if he were picking his words out of a minefield. 'He said, if I had a go at it, I should take a friend. So I said you might come.'

'Oh you did, did you?'

'And then he said it might be even better if I took a girl. It didn't have to be a girlfriend.' Simon screwed up his face, trying to remember the exact words. '"Two young men can look as if they're up to something. A boy and girl might look as if they're up to something too, but not anything that's likely to worry security." Something like that.'

'You didn't . . .'

'No, of course not. But he did ask if you had a sister. She's just a kid, I told him. I couldn't take her. Anyway, David'd kill me.'

'I sure would.' David felt one of his spurts of rage coming on. 'Simon, *who is this guy?*'

But Simon was shutting himself off again, eyes vacant, his mind apparently deep inside his streusel.

David got up and grabbed him by the shirt. He shook him. The streusel shot off into a corner of the room. 'Just concentrate on *me* for a moment. Answer my bloody question, why don't you?'

Simon stared up at him, startled; even flinched back. But still he didn't say anything; still he didn't tell him.

'And don't even *think* of taking Susie.'

chapter]

'WHERE'S SIMON?' IT was Susie, back hot and sandy from the beach.

'He's gone off.'

'Not like food, I hope.' This was their mother.

'Both meanings,' said David. Simon had become such a secretive bastard. You couldn't even *bully* the truth out of him.

'Greg's really interesting,' said Susie, 'and *friendly*. He does heaps of things. He made me feel dull.' She ticked the 'things' off on her fingers. 'He's done white-water rafting and mountain climbing and he and his friends ride motorbikes all over the place.

To Brisbane, Perth, you name it. And now,' (here she paused impressively) 'now they've picked up abseiling.'

Her mother looked up from her work. 'Is that where you hang out over cliffs or buildings or whatever?'

'More or less. They're hoping to make a bit of money out of it.'

'Do dares for people, you mean?' said David. 'Or be a cheaper version of a rescue chopper?'

'No. Something quite ordinary. Window-cleaning, of all things. It's much cheaper to do it with abseilers, better than those window-machine things. But it looks dangerous, so that employers would worry about the risk . . .'

'The expense, more likely. Of insurance.' David picked up one of his mum's stories: about a hospital that gave people diseases. Deliberately. He thumbed through it. But he kept getting views of The House of Records. What Susie had said seemed to link up with it. There it stood, grey and cold, its steps curving. He thought about that first day he'd got a glimpse of Floor 30 in the daylight. What had puzzled him about it? He saw the roomful of computers, yet only one man was at a desk – that had been strange enough; the green carpet, the huge glass windows. He stared at these mental windows. Yes, that was it, perhaps. They were smudged, foggy; just as stained with weather and with birds as the windows of his classroom at school.

The front doorbell rang and Susie leapt to answer it. There was lengthy bright chatter (from Sue) in the passage but David couldn't pick up whose was the other voice. Male, deep, somehow hollow. Susie came back looking flushed and carrying her wallet.

She waved it at them. 'I left it in Greg's car. Wasn't that nice of him to come round? He thought I might need my bus pass for tomorrow.'

'You mean he looked inside it?' David bounded past her, out to the passage.

'You should have asked him in, Susie. There's still some of that streusel.'

35

David raced out the front door. But Greg was already roaring off. 'Blast!' He felt ridiculously disappointed.

Susie came up behind him. 'What d'you want Greg for? I didn't know you even knew him.'

'Oh, just something I needed to ask him. I'll catch up with him again. Is he a good swimmer?' he added, to change the subject and put Susie off any possible scent. She was a terror at making connections.

'Yes.' She smiled. 'He sure looks good in the water. Such a hunk. And he didn't know there was an Olympic pool near here. Says he might drop by for a swim sometimes.'

'Drop *in*, might be best.'

It was Tuesday, just before tea. David was lazing about at the edge of the pool. He sighed. He was sick of thinking about Simon. How could anyone change so much in only a few weeks? He was relieved to see Cynthia and Susie and someone else with them, coming across the bridge that led to the entrance. 'Hi, Cynth.'

'Greg, do you know my brother David? He wants to have a chat with you about something, the mystery man.'

Greg smiled at him, in an off-hand sort of way. He was of a size to fit the voice at the door: older than David, and broader, more filled out. He looked like a lifesaver: confident, graceful, as tanned as it was fashionable these days to be. Susie looked quite small and very young beside him.

David waited till the girls were racing one another up the pool. 'It was about this abseiling, Greg.'

'We got enough guys.'

'Right. It was more the window-cleaning idea I meant.'

Greg stopped looking at the girls and concentrated on David for the first time.

'I was wondering, if you took on a really well known, multi-storey building – in the night – as a sort of stunt, whether it might catch on. For publicity. You could have a poster, *30 storey building takes x hours to clean by conventional methods* . . . What d'you think?'

'Mm. Might work.' Greg thought about it. 'Not easy, though. Security guards. Video cameras. Alarm systems. Police drivin' round the city twenty-four hours.'

'What if the building was out of town?'

'Mm. But what's out of town?'

'The . . . House of Records.'

'No way.'

'Why not?' said David. 'It's perfect. And its windows are streaky. Haven't been done for ages, by the look of them. Although it could be the wind . . .'

'It's high security. All those records they keep about us.'

'But it'd only be a stunt. You'd only be outside. Even if they caught you . . . Maybe it'd be even better if you *were* caught. Think of the headlines.' He drew imaginary words across the air with his finger. 'RECORD CLEAN-UP. Daring young abseilers risk life and limb to restore House of Records. Sparkling windows give building back former profile.'

'Mm. I'll talk to m' mates.'

David could see his sister was getting ready to come out of the pool. She was bobbing around the way they always did after a swim, getting her breath, pushing her hair back behind her ears. Cynth was still swimming like a tank.

'Don't mention it to the girls.'

'I never tell sheilas nothing. What *you* so interested for?'

But before David could work out what to say, the girls were back, giggling, splashing them with bright water from the pool.

chapter 8

SUNDAY. DAVID RUBBED Ged's black head through the palings and waited for someone to come to the door. The bell had rung all right: he could hear it peel sonorously, expensively, up the long hall.

It was Simon's father who at last answered it, looking his old self in gardening shorts and shirt. 'Oh, it's you, David. Come in. Nice to see you. I'm doing a bit of pruning out the back. Like to help?'

'Well . . .'

'Only joking. I know it's Simon you're after. But come see what I've been doing. Then I'll look for Simon. I'm not sure, he might be . . .'

He led David through the vast arched hallway, thickly carpeted, that ended in the kitchen. Its views were of a walled garden. He took David out through the side door. At the back, the garden was unexpectedly small, most of the block lying to the front in smooth lawn and large gums. It was private, though, pleasant, surrounded by a high stone wall with rambling roses all over it in clusters of tiny pink blooms. The grass was dark green here. Moss grew between the grey stones that made a path across it. David looked up at the solid stone of the house. He wondered which bedroom looked out on to this. Simon's view was of the kidney-shaped pool at the side.

'I've been trimming back the creepers. Ivy like this'll go rampant if it's left. I might pull it out altogether, and put in something softer like wisteria or jasmine. What do you think?'

'I like wisteria. The blue kind. I like mauvy blue flowers like jacarandas and agapanthus.'

Simon's father beamed. 'So do I, David, so do I. And it *is* a bit dark in here, isn't it?'

'Yes. Although I like that too. All the different greens. It seems secret.'

'Mm. You might be right.'

David had learnt long ago that the way to Mr Hatherley's heart was through his garden. Not that he minded that. He liked things that grew, himself. It was odd, though, how Simon's dad didn't take better care of his tools. His spades looked as if they'd spent

38

a lot of time hanging about in the rain. Equally odd was why he hadn't called out to Simon first. David turned restlessly and looked up at the house again.

'Right.' Simon's dad took off his gloves. 'I'll go upstairs and see what's going on.'

That seemed a funny way to put it, David thought, as he paced up and down on the tiny stone path. Why didn't he tell him to go and look for Simon himself? He glanced down at his feet. He was sure he looked clean enough to walk up the stairs. Anyway, his dad was dirtier from the garden than he could possibly be thought to be.

'Oh, there you are, David.' It was Simon's mother. 'Simon says he'll come round later, about teatime, if that's all right.' She smiled at him, uncomfortably. 'Can I get you something? A cup of tea?'

Yes, thought David, she damn well could. Why couldn't Simon tell him himself? What was it went on around here anyway? It was like trying to get an audience with the queen to see Simon in his own home. He remembered that day he'd come round and his mum hadn't even let him in the door. Maybe Simon hadn't been out then, either. 'Thanks,' he said, following her through to the kitchen.

She rummaged around in the cake tins, finally producing some rather crumbly-at-the-edges chocolate wheatens. 'And how's school, David? Studying hard?'

David thought about all the maths problems that were still at home, waiting for him, spread out on the table. He'd better try to get them done before Simon turned up – *if* he turned up. If he *wanted* him to turn up. Surely he couldn't still be sulking. It'd been Simon's fault. 'Trying to, Mrs Hatherley. You know what it's like when the weather's nice.'

She seemed restless, edgy, bobbing back and forth in between making the tea, getting the milk out the fridge, mopping up the sink. It all seemed to be taking much longer than it should have. He watched her fussing about.

'Why don't *you* sit down?' he said at last, taking over. 'Let *me* pour *you* a cup.'

'Thanks, David.' She collapsed into a chair. 'Oh. I forgot the sugar.'

'I don't take sugar, Mrs Hatherley.'

You'd think she'd remember, after all these years. They'd often had conversations about it, when stuck for something else to say – not that they'd often been stuck: how they both had sugar in coffee, but couldn't stand it in tea. And about milk, amounts of. How they could take coffee coolish, but tea had to be hot.

'I wish you'd call me Meg now that you're so much taller than I am.'

He smiled, but uneasily. 'I'm not sure I could.' He knew now he wouldn't be able to call her anything, caught unhappily between 'Mrs Hatherley' and 'Meg'. To call someone older by their first name was to turn them into a person, someone you had to think about instead of something that was simply there. He didn't want that. He wondered why it had got so hard to talk to her. Once he could have chattered away. But then Simon was usually here as well, not huddled out of sight upstairs. It was something about this cold stone house, he thought, and shivered. Even on a warm day it was cold inside. It wasn't welcoming, like their place in Ethel Street had been. He remembered the brown and yellow lounge suite and how, one day, he'd spilt his tea on it. 'There's plenty more spills in there, David,' she'd said. 'Nothing to worry your head over.' She hadn't even wiped it up until she thought he wasn't looking.

But now, like him, she sat uneasily in this house, sitting on the edge of the cane lounge, not bouncing around on the failing springs of the old sofa as she had used to do. Maybe that was what was wrong with Simon too: transplanted, to where the soil didn't agree with him either. He stared into his cup, then sipped at his tea, miserably. He felt . . . *lonely*. He stood up when he'd got the level down and when the silence which had fallen around them seemed to have dropped into his cup as well. He smiled at her, as warmly as he could manage. A false, uncomfortable smile. 'Thanks anyway. Thanks for trying,' he meant his smile to say.

Simon was playing with his food. That was all you could call it, David thought, as he watched him endlessly rearranging it. He'd piled the slices of roast lamb neatly on top of one another, and now was positioning his mashed potato in two equal heaps at either end of it. His beans he'd already carried over to the edge of his plate. It looked less, but he couldn't have eaten more than a couple of mouthfuls. He waited to see how soon Susie or his mum would notice, but they were too busy hoeing into their own.

'Can I get some more, Mum?' He'd already taken his plate over and was hacking into the bone.

'Me too,' called Susie. 'You've put honey over it, haven't you? It makes it go that lovely dark way.'

'You put prunes in it once, with bacon,' said David; then added hastily, 'I love it like this, though.' He quickly forked a couple of slices off Simon's plate as he went past and put them with his own. Mum could be such a terrier and Simon didn't want to be badgered: you could tell just by looking at the droop of his shoulders. Maybe what he had to tell him would cheer him up.

His mum licked her knife in a satisfied way. 'Mm, that was nice. Lamb's such a sweet meat, isn't it? And you can never spoil it. It never goes dry like beef will. There's no sweets . . .' (she waited for the faces to fall) 'but there is fruit.' Everyone beamed again, even Simon. 'Grapes and . . . peaches! One each.'

That really was a treat. Peaches were about a dollar each, David knew. They'd been so scarce this season. He gloated over the peaches, mellow, ripe-smelling: yellow where they weren't red, bright red where they weren't yellow.

'Sunset peaches. Visitors choose.' He held out the bowl to Simon, who passed it straight to Susie, who passed it to her mother. 'Oh come on,' she said. 'They're all about the same size and ripeness. I don't care.'

'Then choose one and get on with it.' David could already

41

imagine the juice running down his chin, his teeth nuzzling into the stone.

Simon managed to eat all his peach, David noticed; he even made a dent in the sultana grapes. 'And thanks for the beer,' he said. 'Just what I needed.'

'You've been lashing out tonight, Mum. You and Susie go and watch your serial. Simon and I'll wash up.'

'Oh, would you, boys? Heaven. I'll have a cup of coffee too, after you've finished. Black, with one sugar.'

'Just place your orders.'

'I'd rather have tea.' Susie rushed into the lounge after her mother before the boys could change their minds.

David waited till the sound of the television came through, then he shut the kitchen door. He told Simon about Greg and the abseiling and the window idea. 'Greg says he'll do it.' He paused impressively.

'Good.'

'Good? Is that all you can say? It's great! Let's get a little enthusiasm up around here.'

'No, it *is* good. Great!' But his shoulders still had that droop about them. 'I worry a bit about so many people being involved. I'd rather you'd let me in on it first.'

'That's rich, coming from you. Anyway, you haven't been around. And it's only Greg and his two mates. I thought you'd be pleased.'

'I am.' But Simon's voice was flat.

'I haven't told him anything. I only said, could he let us know a few days before. We'd like to come and watch, and it might need a bit of planning.'

'What if he doesn't? Let us know, I mean.'

'He will. He knows it's important. "I kind of get this feeling you guys are up to something." I just laughed, but in a way that would let him know he was right.'

chapter 9

SATURDAY. IT WAS a hot night, clear and still, the sky huge and heavy with stars. Two o'clock was to be the time, the dead time of the city; certainly the dead time of a suburb like this. Even by five, even on a Sunday, the cars would be starting up again.

David felt irritable and out of sorts. It would all be a waste of time: there'd be no one working back on a Saturday. They'd had to leave Simon's at 3 pm in order to get to The House of Records well before it closed. They were supposed to be meeting some friends and going to the movies. Actually, they'd spent a lot of weary time just sitting in the car. To cap it all, they'd had another fight.

Simon had mentioned 'this guy' again.

David felt like punching him. 'If you talk about him once more without saying who he is, I'll bash your head in. Who *is* this guy who knows everything about the rotten place?'

'It doesn't matter,' said Simon. 'It doesn't matter who he is. It's the information that's important.'

'How come you believe in this "information"? You wouldn't believe in it unless it's someone high up. Or someone with access. And who do you know like that?'

But there, it had got back to the same old question. Simon repeatedly stonewalled till David got sick of trying. He even sensed a growing coolness in his feeling for his friend.

The boys were dressed in navy, without white shirts, and had blacked out their faces in the washroom. Simon wore a cap over his bright hair.

The building was starting to seem familiar, almost home-like. David had refused to eat tea in the washroom as before and they'd had it on one of the lower floors. It was clear that Simon's precious informant was right: the security cameras hung in odd places and at odd angles everywhere in the building, yet their

43

own presence appeared to go entirely undetected. Their very safety appeared at times eerie; almost, as if it were allowed. At one o'clock they headed up the stairs.

'We'll get there early,' Simon said. 'Just in case.'

They took it slowly, very gently, and even more slowly on the higher floors, till it seemed for ever they'd been climbing stairs with views, in arrow-slit windows, of the stars. Arrow-slit view 25 had Greg's rope in it. So the 'in case' had happened. Greg and his team were early too. They waited now, in the darkness of the stairs, by Floor 30.

Cautiously, hair by hair, David looked round the stairwell. His heart jumped. There was someone there. A light shone, out of the soft darkness of the room. Not an overhead, but a desk light. An official (perhaps the same one as before) was crouched over a desk tapping away at a computer, a huge print-out rolling steadily from the grey machine on his left.

David looked at Simon, shrugged his shoulders, raised his eyebrows, mouthed 'No go.'

'Not yet, there isn't,' Simon whispered. 'But wait till Greg gets moving.'

On cue they heard the sound of what might be a bucket scraping on cement, then low voices. Almost at the same moment bells rang out on a floor beneath. David pulled back into the shadows, waiting. The official was getting up, was leaving his desk, was peering out of the stained, dusty window. Simon grabbed David's arm and started running down the stairs with his shoes in his hand. He's gone crackers, David thought, but he took off his shoes and followed. Simon had left the stairway and ducked in to the floor below.

'He'll come down to see what the fuss is about.'

'So what?' said David.

'He might use the stairs.'

David thought how dumb he'd been not to think of it. He'd just assumed that the official, God in His Wisdom, would use the lift. But the lift *was* coming down. They heard the familiar faint hum of it and saw the red light flashing for a lower floor. David dropped his shoes and dashed up the stairs with Simon not far behind. What a chance for them! But they wouldn't get more than a few minutes, at most.

The official had been updating what looked like highly personal files, then doing a print-out. They were lucky. They were even lucky that he'd been there. It looked as if he'd got as far as 'V'. Lucky again. David left the top third or so for Simon and took the rest to a desk behind. There was no light there, but he'd brought his torch again. He concentrated on finding the 'P's. *Page, Paget, Partington, Partridge, Paton, Pavey, Peal, Pearce* . . . There it was. He started to feel sick. And such a big list. His torch was flickering. Blast, he should have thought to put in new batteries. Its light was certainly fading. He switched it off, knowing it would come on again, faintly. For a moment he hesitated. He didn't have to look. It was better not to know; he knew that already. But, slowly, almost without his volition, his fingers were straying to the switch. The light flickered on, and in its faint, greyish light he found what he wanted. *Pearce, David. Juvenile.* He skimmed over his details and read across the sheet for the due, for the terminal date. His eyes could hardly take in what they saw. And the lift was humming again.

'Simon,' he called, as loudly as he dared. Simon had spread his sheets all over the official's desk and was sitting quite still. 'Simon. He's coming back!' He grabbed Simon's print-out, sorted the sheets into roughly their original shape, put his own underneath them and headed for the stairs.

He bundled himself down them. How had he got involved in this dumb idea? In any case, who in his senses would want to know? He'd just got pulled along with it all, as if it had been a game. And why had it been so easy? Why had *these* particular files been out? He felt numb, but with an edge of fear.

'Don't forget your shoes,' hissed Simon, his voice sounding husky, unlike itself.

David picked them up on the floor below, and skidded down

the next flights. He belted past Floor 26 where the commotion with the abseilers was still under way, then down the remaining winding stairs, his body shaping into the curve of them, and straight out to the door of the main entrance.

It was locked, of course. But he could hear voices outside, voices of people about to come in. He ran back to the foot of the stairs, looking for Simon. What was keeping him so long? They had left together. Here he came now, round the last curve. He was staggering, clutching his side.

'You okay?'

Simon nodded. 'A stitch,' he gasped.

The lights seemed strong in the main foyer. David looked up at them. The noise outside was increasing. It seemed safe to talk. 'We might get out in all the commotion if we hang around here.'

Sirens wailed, and, through one of the frosted windows that flanked the main door, they could make out the distinctive dark blue flashing lights of police cars.

Simon herded David into the toilets.

David looked around the narrow room, feeling caged in, frantic. He couldn't stay here – not for a whole night, not for a minute, not with the surveillance camera staring blandly down at him. His gaze fell on the cupboard door. That was it. That was what they'd have to do.

He wrenched its door open. 'Clean your face up. Now, grab a bucket and mop. Christ! No one's going to notice if there's water in it! Come *on*!'

They were waiting, fully armed as cleaners, when the front doors burst open and the foyer exploded into sound. It was quite easy for them, Simon first, dressed in his cap and harmlessly bearing bucket and mop, to walk out the door as if they had a perfect right. All David had to do was follow. Even if he had a bit of black left on his face, who was to see it, or seeing it, care? Outwardly calm, they washed the top steps of The House of Records. Above them, on their ropes, Greg and his crew still hung safe, high over the city.

part TWO

'He knows now. Simon. Knows twice, as it were. Or thinks he does.'

'"Thinks"? You mean . . . ?'

'Let's stick to "knows". Knows what will happen.'

'What will happen? What will it do?'

'We'll have to see.'

'You mean just sit here . . . ?'

'Yes.'

'And the other one? What about the other one?'

'You mean . . . ?'

'His friend. The one who was with him. Who else could I mean?'

'Ah. His friend. David.'

'What about him?'

'You're interested in him too? Well, we'll just have to see. We'll just have to see there, too.'

chapter 10

DAVID FELT NUMB for days. He walked around in a mist, only half-hearing what went on around him. Voices, even, seemed to come at a distance. He failed miserably, unexpectedly, the mid-term exams. 'It's no wonder, David,' said his home teacher. 'You just haven't been with it recently.'

Gradually he started to fill with anger: anger against Simon first of all, for getting him into this mess. He hadn't wanted to be part of it. He hadn't wanted to go to The House of Records. Then the anger started to generalise, to turn against everyone and every-thing around him. Even cupboards annoyed him, when they wouldn't pull open at once. He managed to wrench a handle off one in the kitchen. His mother was amused, if anything. 'Not David but Goliath. You don't know your own strength.'

People seemed to be calling him incessantly by his name, as if anxious to placate him. Teachers, classmates, his mother, Susie. Even his father had 'Davided' him over the phone. But he didn't want, wasn't able, to be placated. He found that people irritated him, particularly when they were being nice. Even then, they expected more from him than he was prepared to give. It amazed David that they reacted to him much as they had always done, seeming to be completely unaware that there was a vast hole inside him where he had used to be. He wanted to be left alone. Especially he didn't want to see Simon. Fortunately, Simon seemed to have no greater a desire to see him.

It was Susie who noticed it first. 'Simon coming today?' she asked.

'Don't think so.'

'Why not? He's usually over here Saturday and he wasn't round during the week.'

David said nothing.

51

'Want me to nip over on my bike, see what's going on? It might cheer you up. It's no trouble, I'd like the ride.'

'No. Leave it.'

But the next Saturday, when he still hadn't come, Susie had gone off in search of him.

She came back, looking troubled. 'He promised to come over tomorrow. He seems pretty down. Maybe, not well. P'rhaps *that's* why he's not playing footy.'

'Simon's always a bit pale,' said their mother. 'At least he's always a bit pale lately.'

'Doesn't eat properly,' said David.

'You're not eating properly yourself. Moody teenagers. I don't know. I thought we were giving all this heavy stuff a miss. Not in love?'

'No, Mum.'

'Maybe you should go to the doctor. Have a blood test. It's just possible to have a mild case of glandular fever and not know about it. Maybe Simon had it first . . .' David's mother smiled at her quick solution to not only David's, but Simon's malaise as well.

'Drop it, Mum. I don't need a doctor.'

But afterwards, thinking about it, he thought perhaps it wasn't such a bad idea. Maybe there *was* something wrong with him, something *really* wrong, and if they could catch it early . . . But then he didn't feel ill, or not that kind of ill. The kind of ill *he* felt, came from his head.

On Sunday, when Simon did come, he felt wary, cautious, and Simon was quiet, uncommunicative with him. They'd gone off to the pictures where it didn't show if you didn't talk – was even better. At interval, David bought them each a jumbo (the chocolate-covered cones they'd always had when they were younger). He *felt* younger. He was finding it comforting to lick and chew on things as if he were a small boy again.

He did ask on the way home, 'At The House of Records. Did you get a chance to . . .?'

Simon cut him short. 'Yes.'

'It was all right, was it?'

'Oh yes.' His tone was curt, not inviting further questions. 'And you, of course?'

'It was all right too. Pretty all right.'

'That's good, then.'

Simon didn't question him further, not even about the 'pretty'. You'd think any decent friend would have picked up on that. Not that he'd have told him anything. Who wants to be pitied? Instead he asked, 'How come there was nothing in the paper about the abseiling? Seems odd.'

'What? Oh, that. I'd almost forgotten about it. I guess they wouldn't have wanted that sort of publicity for The House of Records. Might have given other people ideas – more successful ones. Haven't you seen Greg since?'

'No.' He hadn't been around either. Really everything had gone a bit quiet lately, as if the world had lost its sound-track. He tried to pull himself together; even, to sound a bit friendly. 'Want to come in and have some tea?' It would please Susie at least. 'It's Sunday. Should be something decent.'

'No. Thanks. I don't really feel up to it.'

There didn't seem much to feel up to, having a bit of tea with old friends. Still, David was just as glad. He'd had enough of Simon's odd moods.

He watched him drive off. Susie had come down the path and was looking at him, contemplating him perhaps. 'What you thinking about?'

'Nothing much.' About how long I have to live, he could have said. And if it's true. Could there be some sort of a mistake?

'"Nothing much" is making you pretty miserable. Can I help?'

'I wish you could.' It was the first concession he'd made. 'But no, there isn't.'

'It's something to do with that dare you've been having with Simon, isn't it?'

'What dare?'

'You've both been up to something for weeks, always together, always staying the night at his place. Shutting up, when I walk in. Then suddenly, *bang*. You stop seeing each other. Something went wrong. It was Simon's idea, wasn't it? What went wrong?'

'Nothing. It went very well. I suppose you could say it was an astonishing success.'

'Then why the long face?'

'You know how you go a bit flat after something like that.'

'And you're not still to get into trouble over it?'

'Don't think so. Don't care much. Would have happened before now. Nothing's happened.'

'Come for a walk with me, then. There's time before tea.'

They'd taken the car to the beach. The light was subdued, the sea and sky grey. The people were subdued too, at the close of the weekend, not cheerful as David knew they would have been that morning. Even the dogs were subdued, most of them demurely on leads, not acting like their normal beach selves at all. Still, it was soothing, walking here on the silken, cool sand with Sue, staring ahead to the jetty. She didn't talk, but just kept pace with him, slowing when he slowed, giving support with her silence.

He looked out to sea. The sea that was always calming, calmed him. The tide washed in and out, nudging the seaweed, gurgling, whispering, slapping; it would keep on, in and out, no matter what happened to people on the shore. That was terrible in one way, but comforting in another. The tide had a kind of after-sound, he thought, as some things have an after-taste. He liked to think that Susie at least would still be here, looking steadily out to sea as she did now. That comforted him. The numbness faded a little. He wondered, almost, if he could tell her. But it still seemed like something raw, shameful, that had to be tucked away. Like a sore or a contagious disease or even a crime. The effect was the same. If it were known, it would separate him off from everybody, even, especially, from Sue.

He'd been staring down, making circles in the sand with his foot.

But as he looked up, he became aware of someone . . . of someone glancing at him, he had started to think. Now he changed it to 'looking'; looking at him. *Staring*. There seemed to be something faintly familiar about the man, although he wore shorts and a T-shirt which was not how David believed he had appeared to him before. The man seemed oddly out of place on a beach. The 'something familiar' was something, David thought, about the man's eyes. They were of an astonishing blue: an astonishingly bright, but cold blue. David felt a little shiver run up his back. He knew he had seen eyes like these, *those* eyes, somewhere before.

chapter 11

MONDAY. IT'D BEEN Hopkins, in English. G. M. He'd never had much time for him before – all that *Glory be to God for dappled things* stuff. A bit sentimental; a bit twee. Although his teacher, old Western, raved on about him. But the poems they were looking at today were different: strong and bleak and dark. He could understand them almost straight away. You wouldn't think a priest would suffer like that; sheltered, enclosed in stone walls. He had a sudden image of the Hatherleys' house. Worse, to feel like that would be a sin. The sin of despair. The ultimate sin. His teacher had talked to them about that. It seemed hard, making despair out to be a sin, on top of everything else. He didn't think it was quite despair he felt himself, for he still edged it with hope. Not religious hope, but the hope it was all a mistake.

He'd heard about words leaping out at you from the page, but that had seemed such a cliché, so unlikely. But when they came to the lines about the cliffs, the words had glowed for him in a kind of mental dark green:

O the mind, mind has mountains; cliffs of fall
Frightful, sheer, no-man-fathomed. Hold them cheap
May who ne'er hung there.

'Are you with us, Pearce?'

'Sir?'

'What do you think Hopkins is trying to say? Or rather, what *is* he saying that *we* are trying to unravel?'

David shuddered. They were dark words. He read them through again. 'He's saying it's worst inside your mind. That the mind has mountains, but only so that it can have cliffs, where you try to hang on, inside your mind. Only people who haven't felt what it's like can rubbish you about it.'

Mr Easterby looked at David in a surprised way. 'Mm. That's interesting. I'm not sure about the mountains, though. Is that how we're meant to see them? Interesting, anyway. *Good*. It shows that sometimes close attention can look like inattention.'

He should know: he was the one who often seemed to be looking coolly into the middle distance but all the time you knew he was really looking sideways at you. There had been another person who'd looked at him like that.

Somehow, reading Hopkins, knowing that someone else had felt the same way, made him feel better, more optimistic. He tried to think in terms of positive action. Maybe there were ways of avoiding one's fate. He decided to go up to the doctor's.

He hadn't been sure whether to make the appointment with Dr Constance or with Dr Williams. Even getting the chance to make the appointment was difficult enough. As soon as he thought his mum was out of earshot, Susie would appear, and vice versa. And then, of course, there was still the problem of which doctor to ask for.

Dr Constance was young and cheery, almost giggly, with blond hair and a busy, lopsided kind of a walk. Dr Williams was older, greyer, serious – even morose. He was more used to Dr Williams, if you could ever get used to someone like him, but he liked Dr Constance better. She'd come to see him when he'd had those awful stomach cramps. He'd thought he was dying. But the mere look of her, shambling yet busy, made him feel better. 'The old tummy virus,' she'd said. 'Half Goodwood have taken to their beds in agony. Just keep up the fluids. Lots of lemonade, eh? You won't mind that.' She'd laughed cheerily. Beset by virulent wogs but still happy. Nevertheless, out of loyalty and perhaps too because Dr Williams talked about 'stomachs', rather than 'tummies', and didn't speak to him generally as if he were a kid, he'd booked himself in, on such a serious occasion, with Dr Williams.

Tuesday. He announced himself at the desk, then sat down uneasily in the waiting room. On a brown chair. The carpet that he stared at was also brown. Even the flowers . . . He glanced cautiously around. The room was filling up with fellow 'waiters'. He didn't suppose they could rightly be called 'patients' until they'd been classified. 'This patient is sick, this waiter is well', and so on. Most of them, he thought, looked like patients. If he weren't ill yet, he soon would be. Viruses were almost visible. Used-looking handkerchiefs or giant tissues were spread out, ready, on several knees. A child of about four had a thick cold and looked disgusting. The level of dress wasn't high. People looked as if they'd been lying down, and had got up, crumpled, to keep their appointment. There was only one dazzling exception (apart from himself): a girl or young woman who'd come in just after he had, dressed beautifully in blue. Her head was bent, in what seemed a purposeful way, over a book, yet she seemed to be staring only at its cover. He waited, wriggling about in his brown chair, watching as various patients (or 'waiters') were swallowed up into the system.

He noticed how Dr Constance's patients came out looking better; all Dr Williams's looked worse. Of course, you *could* say that people went to Dr Constance with light things, like colds, and kept the really heavy stuff for Dr Williams. But he doubted it.

This first visit was reasonably okay. He'd asked for a check-up, and when he did all right on that, he said he wanted blood tests, the lot, 'just to be sure'.

The doctor looked at him. Lengthily. 'Sure of what?'

Other doctors would have questioned him further. Found out if he needed a clearance for a football club, the army, a job, perhaps. But Dr Williams had asked only the one question, and hadn't pursued it when it didn't produce an answer. Suddenly, David realised that was what he liked about him: was why he'd chosen him. He wasn't a *spying* kind of a doctor. But he was capable of getting angry, or close to it, if he were kept too much in the dark.

Friday. As David waited on his second, follow-up visit, he watched the door opening and shutting on both doctors' patients. Dr Constance's were still easy to recognise. They streamed out light-heartedly, holding on to their prescriptions as if they were recipes for happiness. He could tell which were Dr Williams's too. They trundled out: self-absorbed, depressed, anxious. No easy cures there. He knew *he* must have looked the same when he came out, even though, or especially since, there was absolutely nothing the matter with him.

'Your blood tests show nothing abnormal.' Dr Williams sounded as pleased, as animated as he ever allowed himself to be. 'Cholesterol low. No sign of infection. Iron levels good.'

'Oh.' David knew his voice sounded flat, but he felt too disappointed to pretend. A certificate of perfect health.

Dr Williams gave him one of his long looks. 'Do-you-want-to-be-ill-lad?' The words came out linked, in a single, cold blast.

They got David to his feet. 'No. No, of course not. Thanks.'

Dr Williams got up too from behind his desk. David noticed how he had dark patches under his eyes, as if it were *he* who should have been somebody's patient. The doctor walked down the passage with him, in uncompanionable silence, more to pick up his next patient than to see David out. Perhaps, David thought, he hadn't been a patient at all. Or maybe hypochondria would count as a disease, and Dr Williams might think he had that. He imagined him filling in his card with today's date on it: 'Hypochondria?' Perhaps even without the question mark.

David stood, discarded in the waiting room. There was no sign today of the girl in blue. He wondered about her book: if she'd got past the cover. If this were one of his mum's stories, the girl in blue would turn out to be significant. He sighed, and without the comfort of a prescription in his hand, walked out of the absurdly heavy door and into the street.

chapter 12

SUNDAY. 'YOU'RE COMING with me today.' David's voice was hard, brittle. 'It's my turn. My turn to set up a dare.'

Simon said mildly, 'I'd meant to do something else. But I suppose it can wait.'

'You bet it can wait. I want to do this dare *now*.'

'Okay, keep your hair on. I'd better get a jacket.'

'And your rollerblades.'

'We going up to the Centre?'

'You'll see.'

David drove in silence up Cross Road then turned off at the Toll Gate, headed up the freeway.

'Stirling?' Simon ventured. 'Hahndorf? There's a good big bitumen patch at the back of the shops at Stirling.'

'There's an even better patch where we're going.'

Simon looked sideways at him. 'You okay?'

''Course. Why?'

'You just sound a bit grimly. Heard from your dad?'

'Nope. Haven't had one of his sickening little epistles for ages.'

'You *do* sound odd.'

David pulled in to the car park at the back of the Eagle on the Hill pub.

Simon looked around at the space. 'Hardly big enough, is it? Especially with so many cars.'

'This isn't what we're using.'

'Oh.' Simon pulled on his skates in an abstracted sort of a way.

David rolled out to the freeway and looked down the steep, curling length of it.

'You don't mean . . . ?'

'Down to the Toll Gate,' said David. 'Bet you on how long it'll take. Reckon ten minutes at the outside.'

Simon stared at him. 'Your *last* ten minutes, you mean. You've got to be crazy. Talk about a suicide trip! I know it's Sunday, but . . .'

'It's a dare, okay? Let's go.'

He thought Simon would simply follow him once he pushed off, but Simon was gesturing him back. He turned in a vicious circle, scattering the pebbles at the side of the road.

'Look, Dave, I'm not fit enough. Not up to it. Let's leave it for now.' He sounded almost craven.

'A sort of delayed dare?'

'Yes, if you like.'

'No. Sorry. You put me off delayed dares.'

'So that's what it's about.'

'It's not *about* anything.'

'You're blaming me for failing your exams.'

''Course not.'

'Then why? Why d'you want to do it?'

'It'll be fun. Think of the acceleration. The adrenalin rush.'

Simon shivered. 'What about a beer in the pub instead? They've got a fire going.'

'Afterwards.'

He moved off, not wanting to hear more, and flew across the road. When you stood there, looking down, the road seemed a lot steeper than it ever did from the car. A sharp wind blew through his shirt, and his face tingled in the cold. This time he didn't even look to see if Simon were following. He could come or not as he wished. Simon was the one who'd called *him* yellow, before they'd gone to The House of Records that first time. Let Simon be as yellow as he liked.

David was gathering speed fast as he rounded the first bend. A feeling of power, of pure joy shot through him. He watched the trees rush past against the hills, muted green in the grey light of afternoon. He was even gaining on the car in front. If he could only creep up on it. Dangerous, though who needed to be careful now? But he didn't need to catch it up. A maroon car shot past him, crazily braked, then drew in, in front of him. He lengthened his action, at the same time crouching over more, slanting in to the curves. The driver (a woman) still seemed erratic, speeding up suddenly, then cracking down on the brakes around some of the curves. He pulled in nearer, feeling goose bumps break out all over him. This could be it, getting in as close as this. At least, normally, it could be.

Here it came: he was getting caught up in the hot wave of the car. He moved in even nearer, to what could only be a couple of metres behind it. He stood straighter, took shorter strides, but was travelling far faster than before. Maybe 80 ks. His hair blew back; the exhaust of the car puffed out his shirt; he shouted with joy. As he rounded a bend he caught a glimpse of Simon, trailing well behind, bent over into the wind. Long and thin. Spiderman.

'Wheeee,' he called out, childishly, fleeing another bend, keeping close to the car in front, forgetting for the moment what a hopeless driver she'd proved to be. He was taken up with the whole scene – the twisting road, the green verge, the red gums blowing crazily in the wind – letting it sink into his mind. Far too late he noticed bright, acute red, the red of her brake lights, and in the same second the car in front grew bigger, seemed to be reversing at full speed. He shut his eyes into red darkness, waiting for the inevitable thud. But when he opened them, he was still wobbling along on his skates. She must have accelerated sharply out of the bend. He let her get ahead, waiting for the shock of what had nearly happened to hit him. Here it came. His legs began to wobble, and now his teeth chattered unhappily against one another.

That must be what it was like to die: the car rushing

backwards, the blur of green, a huge circle of pain. Then black-out. Nothing.

Strangely, the episode wasn't able to destroy his mood. Soon he felt another strong fizz of exhilaration, and, as he rounded the next curve, he was looking out for another car to ride.

David could see Simon was actually shaking as he took off his blades, rolled off his socks. David watched, almost pleased. 'Have a good ride?'

Simon said, not looking up, 'It was bloody awful. And you didn't help. D'you realise how close you came to getting cleaned up?'

'Well, I didn't. It was all okay.'

'You were damn lucky.' He picked up his rollerblades and stared up the slope. 'How're we supposed to get home?'

'How d'you think?'

This time David *did* feel the cold of the wind, in a way that was no longer pleasant. The road seemed unbearably long, going back. Simon trailed behind. David didn't stop to let him catch up. He thought Simon was sulking, lagging behind on purpose. But when Simon eventually got back to the car, he could hardly hold himself up, could hardly wait for David to unlock the door.

David looked at him without pity. 'What about that beer?'

Simon stared at him, white-faced.

'Don't tell me. You don't really feel up to it.'

chapter 13

DAVID DIDN'T SEE Simon all week, not that he expected to. But Simon had come round on Friday, though not to talk to him.

'Where's Susie?' David asked when he got home, a bit late, from school.

'Off somewhere with Simon, I think.' His mum was deep in a manuscript, dictionaries and reference books scattered all around.

David wondered whether to say anything, and then found he couldn't stop himself. 'Isn't she seeing rather a lot of Simon lately?'

His mother looked up, reluctantly. 'She always does, doesn't she? He's been round here most weekends since you were in primary school together.'

'I suppose so,' he said, at the same time knowing there was something different about the 'seeing' now.

'Don't make something out of it, David.' His mum spoke quite sharply for her. 'You'll spoil it. You'll make her self-conscious. They're only friends, I'm sure. But it's a friendship that means a lot to her. Simon's always treated her on equal terms – not as somebody's kid sister. Anyway, she's far too young. Simon knows that.'

David wondered if he did. He remembered that look he'd caught Simon giving her. Appraising. Indeed on equal terms. And Susie had grown secretive.

When she got home, he asked: 'What are you and Simon always talking about these days?'

'Oh, nothing much. This and that,' she'd said, very cool, very casual. But then she'd spoilt it all, given herself away, and blushed.

On Saturday Simon came round, this time to see David, and behaved just as if nothing had happened between them. Maybe nothing had, for him.

He'd wanted to watch the local football match.

'Why don't we go see *your* footy team?' David suggested.

For some reason he hadn't wanted to do that.

But by half-time Simon had had enough. 'I don't want to watch. I just want to bloody *be* out there.' He kicked at the turf.

David felt his sourness fade away. 'Maybe you should . . .' Go back to it, he'd meant to say, but stopped himself in time. He hated to be 'shoulded' himself. It was up to Simon. He had to be content with giving him a friendly slap on the back.

Now they were walking along the pavement opposite the shops on Goodwood Road. Simon pressed the button at the pedestrian crossing, then wandered off to look at the church behind them. The light turned green.

'Come on!' called David, then walked away himself when Simon didn't come. They both stood watching, over by the church, as the cars stopped for no one walking across.

Simon laughed. 'It looks strange, doesn't it? Imagine if you were a Martian, looking on, how funny earthlings would seem. Stopping, in rows, for nothing.'

'Let's try it again. There's another crossing with lights, and it's a double one.'

Simon was already running towards it.

They pressed for one crossing, and then, as it turned green, pressed for the other. Again no one else was waiting, and again the cars pulled up in rows. Both boys were laughing helplessly as they raced up and down the pavement, stopping cars at will.

'I'll show you something else,' said Simon. He led the way into a small, rather shoddy-looking supermarket. He grabbed a trolley. 'Just put in anything you fancy.'

'I've only got five dollars on me.'

'Doesn't matter. Pile it all in.'

Methodically, they went round the shelves, pulling off bottles of drink, packets of nuts and dried fruit, chocolate bars, a large packet of cigarettes, a hot chicken. They topped the trolley up with apples, pears, bananas, avocados and then with some things out the freezer: icecream, cheesecake, apple-and-blueberry pie.

'Mm,' sighed David, for the fumes of the chicken were making him hungry. 'How're we going to carry it all? *And* pay for it. Hope you're loaded.'

'Not exactly. Now, wheel the trolley into this little dark corner here . . . Right. You can take one thing out. What d'you want the most?'

David's stomach was still rumbling hopefully after the chicken. He picked it out from under the fruit and waved it aloft.

64

'Not the cigs? Okay, then. Give it to me.'

'You mean we're just going to leave it all? Fair go. What about the frozen stuff?'

'Oh, they'll notice soon enough.' And Simon strode up to the counter.

They took the chicken across the road, giving the cars a proper reason to stop this time, and headed for the church. 'I saw a good spot to sit down in,' said Simon.

'The good spot' turned out to be a tiny graveyard, tucked in behind the church, with graves of grey stone fighting it out with tall shining grass. They sat down together on a long smooth slab. Simon edged the chicken out of its foiled bag and tore a leg off for him. David thought he'd never been so hungry, never enjoyed anything so much. Soon nothing was left but bones.

He patted the warm stone. 'When you die, d'you reckon that's it?'

The words hung in the air.

'Let's not spoil a good day,' said Simon.

'Seriously.'

'I can't imagine any sort of afterlife that makes sense.'

'Me neither.'

'Could you play footy, for example? And what sort of shape would you be in? It might be nice to return as a butterfly or some-thing,' Simon added, watching one alight on the gravestone next to them, 'but the odds against it seem pretty high.'

'And then we're born out of nothing, why shouldn't we just die into nothing?'

'Exactly. I don't think there's much future in it.' Simon pulled his mobile out of a jacket pocket.

'What you doing?' asked David, lazily.

'Calling a taxi.'

'What we need a taxi for?'

'We don't. We just need to call one.'

Simon dialled one taxi company, giving the church as the pick-up point. Then he dialled another. 'Let's see which comes first.'

'What we going to do with two taxis? One each?' David spluttered with laughter.

'We'll just hide till they go away. It'll give them something to do.'

They stood waiting, out of sight at the side of the church, and watched as their taxis, arriving almost simultaneously, cruised up and down the street, then accelerated off, far faster than they should.

They ended up in the pub on the corner, playing the pokies then sitting down with a beer. David had really enjoyed the day, just the two of them messing around as they'd done when they were kids. But now, as he looked out onto the street, thinking of all the bright cars stopping for nothing, the taxis stopping for nothing, he felt himself shiver. Stopping for nothing: almost as if he were a ghost already.

chapter 14

MONDAY WAS A holiday for the school, although not a general holiday. David felt at a loss. Susie had gone off somewhere with Cynth, and Simon was of course at school. Usually they spent their holidays together.

For days now he'd been dreaming about The House of Records. In the dream (for it was always the same one) it appeared distorted: more like a castle or fortress or even a giant church, with interminable straight corridors leading to endless spiral staircases. He would like to see it again, to see it as it really was. He knew he would never get another chance to look at the documents, but he *would* like to see if there really were a floor 30.

He'd tried to talk to Simon about it. 'When we were at The House of Records . . .'

Simon looked away.

'What we found, it was on Floor 30, wasn't it? The one not marked in the lift?'

'Yes.' His 'yes' was abrupt, not inviting further comment.

He studied Simon's shut face. 'Are you sure it was okay, what you read off against your name?'

'I told you it was, didn't I.' His voice was flat, not suggesting a question.

'I'm glad.' And he did feel genuine relief flood through him. 'I just wondered.' *You seem so shut in sometimes, so locked away inside yourself*, he wanted to add. *Or maybe it's more that I feel shut out.* But of course, you couldn't say things like that to your friends.

It was almost as if his mother had been mind-reading. She'd been looking at him, carefully. 'Well. I can think of a nice job for you, to fill in the day.'

'What's that?'

'Get your passport fixed up.'

'What for?'

'Didn't you read your father's letter?'

'Nup.' It had been sitting waiting for him since Friday.

'Really, David.' She pulled it out from under the morning pile of manuscripts.

David turned the letter over, surveyed the stamp, then gingerly pulled out the flimsy sheet. Short, yet fulsome. His father wanted him to go to Singapore later in the year. It would be a business trip for his father, but he'd thought of taking a few days extra if David would go with him.

'Later in the year.' A cold feeling settled in his stomach.

'Better get yourself organised early. I thought today you could get a bus to the records place and get yourself a birth extract. You're sure to want it. You shouldn't need me with you, not just for an extract. I suppose I could write them a note in case.'

He still sat, staring at the letter.

'What's wrong? It'll be a wonderful experience, and your

father's trying to make friends. Give you a treat, get to know you better now you're growing up . . .'

'It's not that . . . The House of Records, did you say?'

'Yes. A birth extract. Really, David. You're so far away these days. And you've got nothing planned. It's a number 30 bus out of the city, the one from Victoria Square. It's the most direct, anyway.'

'"30"?'

'Yes. There's nothing odd about that, is there? Take your driving licence and student card as ID.'

So the bus was number 30. Was there no end to the weird-nesses connected with The House of Records? Maybe, when he looked up at it, it would say '28', not '30' at all. He hesitated, looking down at the letter. Then, thinking of the bus number, he made up his mind. Perhaps he would sleep better if he went back there. It might make the building and the people seem normal, not fragments of a nightmare that would close in on him quite soon. He was trying not to be, but he was almost touched by the tone of his father's letter. He sounded almost . . . Maybe his father *did* want a fresh start, even if that idea, too, were taking on the outline of a bad dream.

'If you stay, David, you could help me with a pile of teenage romances, since you're interested in plots for those at the moment.' She smirked up at him.

He jogged out of the city on the bus. Everyone in it seemed separate, alone, spending the time staring out of dull smeared windows. The gloom of The House of Records seemed already to have captured its bus. David felt his fragile spirits start to fall.

The bus drove out through Wingfield, depressing at the best of times: dusty and industrial and flat, where telegraph poles seemed to dominate. Even at the road verges, grass had died. He hadn't really noticed the desolation when he'd been with Simon, although that had been a slightly different route. This way there were no trees anywhere, only the grey horizon and the equally

68

grey, featureless landscape. His heart tilted when in the distance he could see The House of Records itself. It rose up, a huge mass of concrete, grey, cold, against the lighter grey of the sky.

He pulled a peppermint out of his pocket and sucked on it vigorously. He looked to see what the girl across the aisle was reading. Certainly not a romance from that cover of spidery hands and a distant mansion. He was sure he had seen it somewhere before. The girl had clear skin and auburn hair. She wasn't wearing cliché green either, but a light rust-coloured shirt that made her look all part of the one piece. Her skirt was long and pleated and in a deeper tone than the shirt. Most of the girls he knew wore jeans. Hadn't he seen her somewhere before? She seemed serious, almost solemn. He wondered what she would look like when she smiled.

The bus stopped at last. He walked through dry leaves to the bottom of the steps. They curved above him like rows of dolphins or giant millipedes. Although his visit was legitimate this time, his heart flipped over as he looked up at the hard grey walls. He wondered about the mops and buckets they'd flung away that night into the shrubbery: about who had found them, what they had made of it.

He bounded up the last steps, to stop himself from running away. Nearly colliding with a grey-suited employee. He intended to do what he had done that first time: go, via the stairs, up to Floor 30, mistaken, supposedly, for Floor 13. But first he wanted to look in on the washroom, to see if it were the same as he remembered it. See if the mops and buckets were back. But when he opened the door, all he could focus on was the eye of the security camera, staring down at him.

He walked across the ground floor alone. The swell of people from the bus had already flowed through. He looked behind him for the girl in the rust-coloured shirt, in case she too, had been in a washroom, staring up at a security camera, but the hall lay empty.

He started climbing the stairs, waiting for the floor to come where ordinary would be replaced by arrow-slit windows that yet largely revealed the view. When he dreamt of the building, it was all nightmarish, out of proportion, except for these windows which seemed to hang in his dreams in golden light, like stained glass in a church. He climbed higher and higher, until he saw, with a sense of relief, the unclouded, arrow-slit window of Floor 25. So Greg *had* been here: he hadn't imagined it.

26, 27, 28. People were coming out of the lift onto the highest floor of all; or at least, the highest they thought was there. David held himself still, counting the people. Five, six, *seven* . . . There she was: the girl from the bus, the girl with the auburn hair.

He moved out of the shadows, followed the girl. She walked straight up to the counter with the smallest queue and waited . . .'elegantly', was the word he thought of. Held herself still; poised, with an easy tension.

David stood slightly outside the line of people waiting, and studied her. She was a real stunner; the closer you got, the more stunning she became. It was her turn now. He tried to fit names to her. 'Rebecca', he thought. No, too staid. 'Alexandra'. Too cool. 'Angela'. Too sweetly sweetly. Yet an 'A' name seemed close. He leaned forward, hoping to hear her give her name and as he watched, she flicked back her hair and looked at him. Anna, he thought.

The official at the next counter was calling him over. David had no idea what this floor was for, what the right questions would be to ask. Floor 28: the top floor. Not likely to be routine, then. Sensitive. Criminal records? He stumbled over. 'I'm waiting for a friend,' he said weakly, and turned away.

He walked out to the lift, then ducked into the stairwell and up to the unmarked floors. It was what he had come for, after all.

The stairs looked different in daylight, less and yet more sinister at the same time: brighter, so less, yet unused-looking, and so more. He climbed slowly, quietly, glad he had worn his sneakers, the rubber hardly making a sound. A bird flew across his arrow-slit view. Floor 29. He felt slightly sick. More slowly still he started to climb up the last stairs. But, foot on the second step, he heard voices echoing up from the floor below, or from the stair-well. Someone was coming after him!

The thought of Simon, cool, reckless, sitting in the official's chair, made him turn back and walk down the stairs. If he con-fronted the official before the official could confront him, it would be physically easier to make up a decent excuse. His stomach in knots, he rounded a corner – and stared into the light grey-brown eyes of the girl in the rust-coloured shirt.

She stood on the steps, looking up at him. It seemed a long time before she spoke: 'You're not meant to be here. You do know that, don't you? These steps lead . . . Well, they lead . . . appar-ently to nowhere much. Escape stairs, basically.'

The words seemed strange coming out of such a mouth, out of such a face. 'Apparently', 'basically'. What kind of language was that? She was older than he was, nineteen, maybe twenty. And when would you 'escape' upwards? She was being evasive, wasn't she? She *knew* where these steps led to. He stared at her, mesmerised, then came to himself and shook the hair back from his eyes.

'No, I didn't know,' he lied quickly. 'It's my birth certificate. I'm maybe going to Singapore with my dad.' The unnecessary words flowed out of him.

'I think you'll find extracts are on a much lower floor. The enquiries get trickier the higher you go. Yours will be quite low down, I'm sure.'

What had her enquiry been, tricky enough to make the top floor?

She was escorting him, firmly, to the lift. 'We'll go down together. I'll find it for you.'

He felt himself getting younger by the minute. He searched the control panel and nearly pressed '13'. Luckily it was glowing orange, already. She asked an official in the lift where to get off. She'd left him there, in a huge hushed queue on Floor 13. He stared after her. She had an interesting walk, elegant and slow, yet with a forward tilt to her head that was quite distinctive.

71

He was surprised, much later, when he finally got to the bus stop, to find the girl (Alison, Anita?) behind him in the queue. The light had already started to ebb.

'I didn't thank you,' he said, 'for setting me straight.'

And she smiled at him for the first time. 'Thank me? Why ever should you?'

When the bus came, she went on up the steps ahead of him and took a seat next to someone already there. Disappointed, he sat in the seat behind. All the way back into town he gazed, on and off, at her hair. Auburn. Glorious.

chapter 15

TUESDAY. 'WHERE'D THE kitten come from?'

A very small, creamy-orange kitten was pawing a tasselled bookmark all over his mum's desk.

'Greg bought it for Susie. Isn't it sweet? "Peaches". What do you think?'

'*Greg*? What's he turned up now for? We haven't seen him in weeks. Where's he been?'

'I heard him tell Susie he had to go away. He didn't want to. Some sort of training session. He didn't say where.'

'*Training* session?' What on earth could that mean? He turned his attention to the other thing that worried him. 'And why the kitten?' He stroked its tiny, bony back. 'You mean he "brought" her a kitten, don't you? Nobody buys kittens.'

'*He* did, apparently. He wanted to get her a really nice little one. She must have said she'd like it. I suppose she must've.'

David thought of all the times he'd wished Greg would come round, tell him what'd happened. Now it seemed almost too late.

And the next day, when Greg did turn up, 'to see how the

72

kitten was getting on', he'd been just as evasive as Simon had become. David rushed to meet him.

'No,' Greg said, 'we didn't do no publicity on it. And they took Brett's camera away.'

'What did they say to you? Did you get into trouble?'

'Not exactly.'

(How could you 'not exactly' get into trouble? Either you did, or you didn't.)

'They were okay, once they knew it was just a stunt.'

David's next question wasn't really any of his business. He tried to frame it tactfully. 'We missed you round the place. Mum says you've been away doing a course.'

He paused, waiting for Greg to fill him in. But Greg didn't say anything, just looked at him, bland.

'Was it to do with your work?'

'A new job I'm taking on,' said Greg. 'Something part-time.'

David knew that recently he tended to imagine things about people, but he was sure, from the set of his mouth, Greg was trying to suppress a smile. Not a pleasant one either. Greg, he thought, looked sly.

'Has he told you where he's been?' David asked Susie later.

'No. I didn't think it was any of my business. He just said he had to go away.'

'"Had" to?'

'Yes, I think that's what he said. I was too busy looking at the kitten to pay much attention. He brought her in a basket tied up with apricot ribbon. Isn't she the cutest thing? Greg got her at Wingfield, at the cat shelter, but he doesn't know how long she'd been there.'

'Not long, I shouldn't think,' said their mother. 'Not a gorgeous little thing like that. What do you think of the true romance, Susie?'

Susie riffled through the pages. 'It's not bad.' She paused, then said hesitatingly, 'But it's not very likely the girl could be in love with the two guys at once, is it?'

73

'I'm not so sure,' said her mother slowly. 'I think it does happen. There are different ways of loving people.'

'Her ways don't seem to be too different.' She paused again, then said: 'D'you think you could be attracted to someone you don't even like?'

'It wasn't like that, though, was it?'

David wondered, vaguely, why Susie suddenly looked embarrassed. She even seemed to be blushing. He'd been waiting to get a word in.

'"Wingfield", Susie. Did you say Greg got the cat at Wingfield?'

You went through Wingfield to go to *or get back from* The House of Records. Maybe Greg had just got back? Or had been visiting it regularly on his 'training' programme? *What were they teaching him*?

'Yes, and it's a kitten, not a cat. Aren't you, little dear?'

To David the whole thing seemed sinister – like the Greeks offering the Trojans that giant horse. He would go round to Simon's, see what *he* thought about Greg suddenly turning up again, from *Wingfield*, bearing gifts.

But Simon was wanting to play *Nightmare*, even recruiting his mum to make up the numbers. 'Might as well. There's time before tea.'

David had always considered *Nightmare* a bit silly. It was one of those games with a board, cards and dice *and* a video, but today the harsh, antagonistic voice of the gamesmaster ('I will send you to the Black Hole') sounded menacing rather than silly.

At the beginning of the game they had to write down their greatest fear. David felt a sense of oppression when Simon, later, read his out: 'long corridors'. David had put 'grey water' and Simon's mother, 'fire'. But it was to Simon's fear that David reacted. The image it gave him was of The House of Records, its blank, anonymous corridors stretching cleanly away.

Later, he'd asked him about Greg. But Simon was oddly hostile, wanting to know about the kitten, what it looked like, what

Susie thought of it. It was only a while into the barrage of questions that David realised, recognising the same symptoms in himself, that Simon was showing signs of being (quite seriously) jealous.

'He's quite an old bloke. I'm not sure I trust him. Your mum should be careful about him bringing Susie presents.'

'It's only a kitten, after all,' he said, taking the opposite view. 'And "the old bloke" would be all of twenty.'

'No, but you know what I mean. Susie's young. She needs protecting.'

David felt, unexpectedly, quite warmly towards Simon. He knew exactly how he felt. But so much for his mum's view of Simon's disinterested, elder-brotherly affection. At least he realised about Susie being young. But then, David thought, he *was* her brother, and yet he had these jealous attacks too. Not really jealous: more worried, concerned.

'But what about Greg going away like that? Could he have been forced to?'

'I don't get you.'

'Well, we didn't see him again after that night . . .'

'Oh, coincidence, I should think. What else could it have been? They would hardly have tied him up, would they?'

'I don't know. Sometimes I feel I wouldn't be that surprised. There's something strange about their whole set-up. More than meets the eye. Like with Greg.' And with *you*, he wanted to add, but didn't want to spoil the feeling of at last having a genuine conversation with Simon.

Riding home, he had that odd sensation again of being watched. When he'd got to Simon's, he'd noticed a dark blue car parked just past the house. Now he was sure it was the same car curving slowly out of a side street and cruising along behind him. He felt vulnerable on his bike. Naked. He chanced a quick look back but he couldn't see in through its windscreen. His bike wobbled. The car was very close and coming faster. Panic seized him. He was going to be sideswiped off his bike. It would look like an accident. He pedalled so fast his knees were hitting one another as he rode off the road and up the nearest driveway. He would ride along the footpath instead. It would be harder to get at him, in here among the Stobie poles. His instinct was to head straight for home, no matter what. The car kept following, but at a distance, and then, as he turned with relief into his own street, it suddenly accelerated, did a U-turn, and headed back to Goodwood Road.

chapter 16

ON FRIDAY NIGHT David had a showdown with Susie about Simon. Simon had come round after tea, but he'd spent most of the time with Susie.

'I thought you didn't like him.'

Susie looked genuinely amazed. 'I've always liked him. I like Simon especially. I think he's great.'

'I mean, like him like that.'

'Like what?'

'You know, all the soft stuff. You said his eyes were too small.'

'Did I? I don't mean . . . not in that way. Did I say he had small eyes? Maybe I was annoyed with him about something. He doesn't really. He's very good-looking, actually.'

'You seem to be with him all the time. And . . .' (here he hesitated, not wanting to acknowledge it, even to himself), 'sometimes you both stop talking when I come up. Like tonight.'

'Yes. Maybe we do.' She looked sad. 'But it's not any of that. That's not the reason. There *is* a reason, but it's not that.'

'Then tell me. Tell me the reason.' He could feel himself getting impatient, a spurt of anger readying itself to come.

'I can't. It's not my secret. I only wish I could.'

'How is it that you know it then and not me? He's *my* friend.'

'He's mine, too, David. I sort of stumbled across it. I suppose I asked him about it in a weak moment – a weak moment for him, I mean. A strong one for me. I didn't really want to know.'

'Know what?'

'Know what it was. I suppose I'd guessed. Or guessed the kind of thing it was.'

'Then why haven't I? Guessed.'

'I'm not sure. Although I was given a clue. But I knew before that.'

'These days you seem to be with him more than you're with me.'

'Hardly. But it's just that he needs me more than you do at the moment. And then, with Cynth being so sick . . .'

'*Needs* you more?' David's voice was anguished. *He* was the one who needed help. *He* was the one who needed Susie.

On Saturday he took the car into the Art Gallery in town. He'd started to haunt the places where he felt safe, like the big easy park at Cleland Wildlife Reserve, the dignified hushed State Library, and the Art Gallery, especially its courtyard coffee shop. The floor was of light-grey slate. Creepers meandered over the bluestone wall that shut it off from the museum on one side and the University of Adelaide on the other. The tables and benches were of red wood, probably jarrah. There was an inside part as well, where you bought the food and drink.

He sat at one of the outside tables with a cappuccino and a slice of banana cake with cream. He stirred the coffee, mixing in the froth and chocolate for a long time before he started to drink it. He was thinking about Simon.

He remembered how once, ages ago, Simon had come round to their house. It was a Saturday morning, too. Early.

'David's gone,' his mum had said to him.

Simon looked puzzled, worried, staring up into David's mum's troubled face.

77

'David's here,' he said, pulling on David's arm and leading him to his mother.

'No. David. My husband. He's gone.'

Not 'left' or 'left us', but 'gone'. 'Gone' was more desolate, bleaker, but without blame.

Simon had rushed over to her then, put his small arms around her. 'I'm still here,' he said.

It had been a grown-up thing for a little boy to do, he thought now. No wonder his mother had always adored him.

It was somehow easier to think of Simon then than of Simon now. But he forced himself to think of him now. Why did Simon need Susie? It was all too hard, if no one would tell him anything. It had all started to go wrong, him and Simon, at The House of Records.

He looked at his watch. He must be getting back. His mum might want the car for shopping. He thought, sipping at his cooling coffee, of his last trip there, of the girl he had met. Of her smile. Her face was solemn, almost severe. He conjured it up. She had a straight nose and her cheekbones showed. But the smile had lightened her whole face. Softened it. He smiled himself, thinking of it. But his smile disappeared when he got home.

'Oh there you are,' said his mum. 'Ready for something to eat? Simon brought croissants. Those almond ones you love, from that shop in King William Road.'

'Yum. Where's Simon?' It would be good to have a talk with him. Perhaps find out about this mysterious reason of Susie's.

His mother hesitated. 'He's gone. He was sorry to miss you.'

'Gone'. The word echoed.

She handed him the white Mulot's bag. He took out his croissant and upended the bag for the almond slivers he knew would be lost inside.

'He's gone to a camp for the weekend.'

'Oh, has he? What camp?'

'Actually, Susie's gone with him.'

'*What?*'

'Yes. I said it would be all right. And Simon had got special permission for her to go. Gone to a bit of trouble.'

'She didn't say anything to me.'

'No. I think she was a bit worried you wouldn't understand.
That you'd take it the wrong way.'

'And *you* bloody understand. *You* don't bloody take it the
wrong way.' Here he was again – on the outside of everything.
A spectator.

'No. He's a decent boy, Simon. I thought it would be good for
her to go. And there's absolutely no need to swear.' His mother
didn't look at him and seemed in a rush to stop talking about it.
'I was wondering, David, if you wouldn't mind taking Peaches
down for her second lot of shots. She had the first lot at Wingfield
a while back. Susie meant to take her this morning. Just go to the
vet on Goodwood Road. There's no need to search out Dr Cole
for a thing like that.'

'Susie can do it on Monday.'

'It's due now, and it's hard to get in at night. Anyway, she'll be
tired on Monday.'

'It's her shitty cat.'

'Oh, come now, David. The cat belongs to all of us. And pick
us up a couple of pieces of porterhouse on the way back. We
might as well treat ourselves since there'll only be the two of us
home for tea.'

Fuming, David went off to the shed to get the cat basket. It
was a solid wicker one. He remembered going with his father to
a shop in Rundle Street, just off the Mall, to pick it up. They'd
bought the best and biggest they could find. His father had been
quite excited about it. They were going to choose a cat together
that very afternoon. He must have been very small because he
had trouble seeing out of the windscreen of the car. He remembered getting the basket almost more than getting the cat. The
cat, from a pet shop, had been called Shadow. It was his father's
choice. Typical of his father, to take him to choose a cat and then

pick one out himself. The cat *he'd* wanted was white. 'Blanche', he'd called it. It had a pink nose.

The basket was sitting ready on the bench. Susie must have got it down from the rafters. He fingered the wooden clothes peg that held the catch across. What had originally kept the catch in place must have got lost or broken, but his father had worked out that a wooden peg, tied to the basket with strong green twine, would function just as well. He carried the basket back to the house. It felt heavy even now. No wonder he remembered struggling to lift it off the floor of the shop all those years ago. He banged it down on the kitchen table. 'Peaches,' he yelled.

'Remember to put something in the bottom, David.' His mother was calling to him from her bedroom. 'An old newspaper will do. And be gentle with her. She'll be frightened.'

David pulled open the door of the basket. There was newspaper in there already, but it was a bit crumpled up. He pulled it out to smooth it. Someone had marked something on the page. He turned it round to have a look.

He stared down at the words. They didn't seem to make any sort of sense. They kept going blurry; in, then out, of focus. He gazed at the picture that went with them. He brought it up closer to his face. It was dotty and indistinct, but there couldn't really be any doubt. Could there? Not when you considered that the picture and the words were ringed around in red.

chapter 11

AT FIRST HE thought it couldn't be true. There had to be some other explanation. Simon must just have gone there, to this earlier camp, with somebody else: a friend who was sick. And then he could see that everything else was starting to fit in, was falling slowly into place. The way Simon had become so evasive; the way Susie was always with him. The 'reason' she had mentioned. 'There is a reason, but that's not it.' Even The House of Records. It was the same reason lying behind the dare. Simon could have left him out of it. He might have left him out of it, he thought, almost angrily. And then felt himself collapse into sadness. He could only have missed it, missed it about Simon, because he'd been so preoccupied about himself. And Simon hadn't really seemed ill. Had he?

In a daze he drove the little cat to the vet's and then home again, picking up the porterhouse on the way. He dumped the kitten and the porterhouse on the kitchen table and then thought better of it and put the steak in the fridge. How was he to get through the whole weekend until he could talk to Susie, until he could talk to Simon? Perhaps he would write to his father. There seemed to be a sudden urgency to do that. But when he sat at his desk and got paper, pen and envelope together, even a stamp from his mother, he found that he couldn't write anything, not a word.

He roamed through the house. 'Mum, where is this camp?'

'I'm not sure exactly.' And then, seeing his face, 'It's on the Victor Harbor road. Don't worry, I've got a phone number for it. Look, David, they wouldn't even *be* there yet. Relax. Give Susie a ring tonight – if you really must.'

'Can I take the car? *Please*.'

She hesitated, but only for a moment. 'All right. I'd meant to stay home anyway. I've got to get through this bundle of work by Monday. There's more coming, would you believe? But be careful.' She studied his face. 'You look a bit, a bit . . . *wild*. Where're you off to?'

He said the first thing that came into his head. 'I might go round and see Greg.'

'*Greg*?'

But when he came out of the drive, he found that he was heading south. He'd guessed where the camp might be: there weren't too many places it *could* be, on the Victor Harbor road. He drove in the wet at speeds that horrified his mother's mild little car. It rocked noticeably and wheezed and rattled so much he could tell the rear shockers were finally giving out.

Rain bucketed down. He altered the windscreen-wipers to fast and drove on at the same speed. Simon must have lied to him: he wondered what fate he really *had* read off that day at The House of Records. Nothing good, he suspected, remembering how at first Simon had seemed just as anxious to keep out of his way as he'd been anxious to keep out of Simon's. How dumb he'd been, yet who could have guessed that *both* of them . . .

He'd taken the broad South Road that led down past all the beaches, but now he swung off it onto the road to Victor Harbor. It was narrower and twisting, but empty, and he drove even faster, the back wheels skidding round some of the sharper corners. He had to find out what was going on, and why he was always being kept in the dark. Especially since Simon had *made* him go to The House of Records. He had to know *now*. Simon *owed* him his confidence. And he'd always been his best friend, hadn't he? Simon had certainly been his. It was Susie who knew. Not him. Even his mum seemed to know, or know something.

He imagined confronting them both. Going up to the door of this hotel or retreat or whatever it was. 'I need to speak to Simon Hatherley,' he'd say. Not 'I want to' – that wouldn't have in it enough authority or desperation. Or could he just walk in, pretend he was someone meant to be at the camp? After all, Susie was there. She was allowed to be there. He could be just as allowed as Susie, he thought childishly.

The road was deserted. Or was it? He'd been so busy inside his head that he was only vaguely aware of what lay outside it. He glanced in the rear vision mirror, and then again. There was a dark-looking car behind him. At a distance, but near enough. It had a rack on its roof. He rather thought he had seen it behind him on the South Road. But there, he was imagining things. How important was he that people should be following him? No one would follow anyone on a day like this, the rain pelting down, the wind gusting. He went even faster, whizzing down slopes, veering into bends. He was coming up to a wind tunnel but he didn't slow down. Nothing could touch him today. The car rocketed across, swaying from side to side. If the car were really following him, he would give it an interesting time.

But the dark car came on, keeping at the same distance, still in the centre of his rear vision mirror. On impulse he swung off the main road and took a side one that would lead south, he thought, to the road his family always took on the way to Cape Jervis. He rushed down the bumpy slope of it, keeping to the middle of its small strip of bitumen. The wind rose as he drew nearer to the sea.

The road was empty behind him. He had imagined it then. After all, other people were allowed to drive to Victor Harbor too. He felt annoyed with himself, and then pleased. He had a picture in his mind of the stretch of road he loved most. The road bordered the sea for only a little way. There were high cliffs on one side and the sea on the other. There was a small strip of beach and rocks and, usually, the tangy smell of seaweed. The sea was framed by a row of pines that grew there unexpectedly as if it were a busy spot like Glenelg or Largs Bay. It seemed strange here, forming a frame or windbreak, here, where there was no one to notice it or need protection.

He pulled in beside a pine tree, where the car would have a nice view while it waited, and tried to open the car door. The wind was pressing against it: he had to push hard to get out. He bent forward against the gale, for that was what it seemed to be here. He walked up the beach, rocking from side to side much as his mum's poor car had had to do over the bridge. Seagulls were calling overhead. Their cry always suggested the sea. Seemed to have the sound of the waves and the wind trapped in it.

The sea itself was empty, the sky heavy and grey. It wasn't raining now, although it would be soon again. The sand was pitted with raindrops, and, even against the wind, he could smell the fresh bitter tang of the seaweed. His hair blew over his forehead, then was pulled back hard in the wind. His face stung. Not *quite* empty the sea, for now he could distinguish a buoy, orangish-yellow, like a giant balloon, surfing on the waters. If he could see Simon here. This was the right place to see him. Not in a calm, polite, protected retreat with other people everywhere around. Even his sister. It was Simon he had to talk to.

There'd be no point in looking for the right road on to Victor Harbor. He felt vague now about where this retreat place actually was. His mind was emptying of purpose. He took off his shoes and socks and flung them on the sand; rolled up his jeans. He had to pick his way through the stones that lay everywhere upon the beach. Suddenly the sand shone up at the water's edge. He traced a line through its shininess. It could be the end of the world here, and he the last person alive.

He was sorry he hadn't managed to write to his father today. I'd like to see him, he thought, not just write to him. Maybe I could go across. He had a bit of money saved up, for a car he'd meant it for. But he wasn't going to need a car; he wasn't going to need the money. What a waste. All that money sitting saved up in a bank. He'd take it out: go to Sydney. Just a weekend would do. It would be a goal, something to aim at. Something to finish off. And he'd love to fly again. In a plane you felt suspended, as if you could stay up there for ever, completely separate from all the mess down below. He would really like that. It would screen him off from what was to happen. It would erect a barrier, a glass wall between time now and time after.

He listened to the seagulls screaming. He paddled in the icy water. The wind came in gusts and blew the fresh scent of the pine trees towards him. He felt his mind go blank and fill up with the sound of the sea.

chapter 18

TREAD SOFTLY BECAUSE you tread on my dreams. David said the words aloud. It was Sunday afternoon and he was hanging about waiting for Simon and Susie to get back from the camp. He'd often seen the line of verse above his mother's desk, knew she put it there to remind her to be kind to her authors. Not that she needed reminding. It had never meant anything to him before. But now he said the words aloud, gently.

'It's lovely, isn't it?' His mother came in, carrying the kitten. 'It's Yeats, apparently. It sounds like him. Early Yeats perhaps, because he was always talking about dreams then. I'm not sure it's quite accurate. I heard the words spoken in a funeral service and I was sure I'd remembered them properly. But I've been right through Yeats's poems several times and I haven't been able to find it. Unless it's in a play.'

'What about the *Oxford Book of Quotes*?'

'It's not listed.'

It worried David that the quotation might not be right. He didn't like to learn it off if it weren't right. He must have a look himself.

'I think that's them now.' His mum rushed to the door, then came rushing back. 'You'll be sensible, dear.'

David tried to be sitting down and at ease when they tramped through, currents of fresh air coming in with them. He could see that Simon looked anxious. 'Hi,' he said, trying to make his voice sound friendly and casual at the same time.

'Stay for tea, Simon,' said his mother, sounding relieved. 'Fettuccine with chicken and mushroom, and peach pie. What do you think?'

Simon grinned. 'I'll stay. Could I just ring my mother, tell her we're back?'

'Of course.'

David could hear Simon protesting about how fine he was, about how slowly he'd driven back. He looked at Susie. She was wearing a parka of mulberry-pink and a checked scarf over her jeans, and had an outdoor, healthy look about her. 'Country Road girl,' he teased.

'Not in a fifty-dollar parka, I'm afraid.'

'So how was the camp?'

'It was all right.'

'Just all right? Too cold? Food no good?'

'No, the food *was* good. Almost as good as Mum's.' She hesitated. 'It was just pretty sad in a way.'

'Sad? Funny sort of a camp,' he said, testing her out. Maybe she would tell him now. 'Why was it sad?'

Susie looked as if she'd said too much already. 'Maybe it was just the way I was feeling.'

'So being with Simon wasn't such a load of laughs?'

'I didn't expect it would be. That's not why I went. I didn't, in fact, go for the laughs.'

David was surprised by the sternness in her voice. Usually she was soft as butter – like his mother. She was being quite cold about it. 'Hey, steady on. I didn't mean anything. What did you think I meant?'

'Okay.' She tried to smile. 'I keep forgetting you don't . . .'

'Don't what?'

'Know when I'm teasing.'

But David knew she'd altered her sentence in midstream. And it wasn't true. He *did* know when she was teasing. Wasn't he one of the only three people who had known her the whole of her life? Even she couldn't claim that of him.

Simon came through at last. 'Mothers!' he exclaimed, throwing himself down on the old sofa. 'Sometimes I think they *like* to worry. It's something to fill their heads with.'

'What a cruel thing to say!' said Susie. 'Imagine how you'd feel if your mother *didn't* worry. *I'd* worry if I were your mum. I worry anyway,' she added, half to herself. But David heard.

Simon ate his way steadily through the fettuccine and even more steadily through the peach pie. 'Could I have some more?'

David's mother was delighted. 'I'm pleased you've got your appetite back again. For a while, there was no pleasing you. I tried chicken fillet stuffed with mushroom, avocado and camembert cheese and you left half of it. And that steak pie with the flaky pastry that melts in your mouth . . .'

'Yum,' said Susie. 'Could we have that next Sunday night? And Simon can come if he promises to eat up a proper share.'

'I think I'm actually putting on weight.'

'Thank goodness for that! You're tall enough, now it's time you filled out. David, have that last piece of pie.'

'I couldn't,' he said regretfully. 'I'm full. *You* have it.'

'Maybe I will. It looks kind of lonely and untidy in the dish by itself.'

Soon after they'd finished eating, Simon pushed back his plate and got up slowly. 'That really was delicious, but I'd better get home.' And, almost shyly, 'Thanks heaps for coming, Susie.'

They all went with him to the door. David didn't get a chance to talk to him. In any case, he could see that Simon had suddenly got very tired. All the colour had disappeared from his face. David followed Susie back inside. He thought he wouldn't ask her about what he'd found in Peaches' basket. He would rather talk directly to Simon about it.

He was pleased to come across Simon, a couple of days later, rather than having to search him out. Now that it had come to the point, he didn't know what to say, didn't know how to introduce tactfully what Simon hadn't been prepared to tell him himself.

Simon was swimming alone in the pool. He wasn't with anybody; indeed the pool was deserted. 'Hi. I was going to come over after I'd had a swim.'

But David doubted it. Simon had come for a swim on his own as he often did now himself. It was funny how this situation forced you back on yourself. It wasn't just that it made you feel shut out, shut out of other people's lives, shut out of life itself. In the end it actually made you *want* to be alone. Once they would never have dreamt of going swimming without each other.

He felt a great wave of sadness roll over him as he watched Simon pounding up and down. But Simon's concentration clearly was broken; he kept looking round to where David stood. He seemed also to keep staring up at the clock. Perhaps he had an appointment? David certainly hoped not. What he wanted to say might take a lot of time: not a lot of time to say, a lot of time to come out.

Simon pulled himself half out of the water. 'You coming in or not?'

'Not.'

Simon swam a few more lengths, on his back this time, gazing up at the postcard blue of the sky. Then he climbed out and sprinkled David's face heavily with water.

'Thanks.'

Simon towelled himself down, then lay beside him.

'Water good?'

'Not bad. Bit of a chilly edge at first.'

David rolled over onto his stomach so that he was staring into the grass. He tried a few openings in his mind. 'I've been wondering about a few things to do with you. About how sometimes your mother says you're out, or I can't see you. Or you don't turn up here for a while.' Too devious. Or, 'I was wondering about what sort of camp it was.' Too direct. Or even, 'I don't feel things are the same between us any more.' He cringed away from that one. Too personal and self-pitying. In the end, the words had started to come out by themselves.

'Sime.'

'Mm?' Simon was lying with his eyes shut, soaking up the sun.

'You're ill, aren't you?' He raced on. 'I found an old newspaper in the cat basket. There was a picture of kids on this CanTeen excursion. Teenagers with cancer. There was one in the background with his face turned away. It was dotty, indistinct. But it was you, wasn't it? Susie had ringed the picture in red.'

Simon opened his eyes but didn't answer.

'Why does Susie know about it and I don't?'

Simon sighed and turned over too. 'I just wanted something to be normal. Things aren't the same at home or school any more. And Susie guessed. I didn't want you to know. I wanted things to be the same with you.'

'But they're not, are they?'

'No. Sorry.'

'Don't be sorry.' He pulled out a few blades of grass and chewed on them, one by one. 'How long have you known?'

'Remember that footy game against Rostrevor? It was just after that.'

'How bad is it?'

'Pretty bad. Although it's funny, I feel as though I'm getting better. I really feel a heap better. And I'm eating again . . .'

'Well, there you are then. You're beating it. You're getting over it.'

'Yeah.' Simon sounded disheartened, defeated even.

'Do the doctors . . . ?'

'They think I'm a lot better. At the moment.'

'At the moment?'

'These things tend to come and go. You think you're getting better; then bang!'

'Just the same, you could think you're getting better and be *really* getting better. Couldn't you?'

'Yes, I suppose so.'

'Then go for it. You're looking great.'

Simon sighed again.

David probed deeper. 'Unless it's got something to do with The House of Records. If you still feel awful, in spite of feeling better, I mean.'

Simon didn't say anything.

'That's why you made the dare, wasn't it? That's why you wanted to go there, to find out . . . But it was okay, wasn't it? You kept saying it was okay.'

'That's what I said.' He was silent for a moment. 'But . . .'

'Go on.'

'It wasn't exactly okay.'

'Does Susie know?'

'Nobody knows.'

'Then tell me. Tell me, Simon.'

The sun had disappeared behind a cloud. Simon sat up. He was shivering. He reached for his damp towel and pulled it around him. The colour, a rich tan, made David think of Alice, Alicia, Annette. Of the girl on the bus whose clothes had matched her hair. He didn't even know her right name.

'Level with me. You made me come with you. I didn't want to come.'

Simon looked down at him out of a white face. Then he looked up at the sky. 'If you really want to know, if you're that rapt in knowing. Due date 14/6/98.' His voice was bitter.

David couldn't take it in. He felt himself collapse into the grass. 'Say it again.'

'I'm kaput. Finished. Now "only a matter of time" means just that.'

'I mean, the date. Say the date on the print-out again.'

'Does it matter all that much? 14/6/98. The fourteenth of June, 1998.' He was almost shouting it. 'How many weeks does that give me? How many days?'

'But you said, you made me think . . .'

'Well, wouldn't you have, if it'd been you?'

chapter 19

DAVID HAD STARTED getting up at odd hours. His mother caught him that morning. He was outside before the sun came up. The sky was blue, threaded with pink, the last stars fading. The trees stood up black against the house, surrounding the TV antennae, equally black. The birds chirped in an early-morning, one-syllable way.

A plane went over, brighter than the stars, tail-light a cheerful red. White light flashed from wing to wing. The sky looked high and far away, but made possible by the plane.

Too soon the black of the world started to colour: became more ordinary, faded to green. Only the antennae persevered. He sighed and turned away.

'Whatever are you doing, up so early? Staring at the sky as if you've never seen it before.'

'I've never seen this one before.' If there were a heaven it would have to be up there. But then, how could anyone over five really believe in that? And it was a way of opting out, wasn't it? Of finding significance in something outside what you knew, instead of in your life as it was. The ultimate cop-out, this way of not facing the reality of your death. And yet, words like *Yea, though I walk through the valley of the shadow of death, I will fear no evil*, seemed to bring comfort, just in the saying of them. He felt drained, as if the day had finished already. But full too, as if already he had had enough for the day.

After breakfast he stood out the front, waiting for Simon. Another weekend. They were coming around so fast. He felt warm now, thinking of him. Warm and sad and puzzled at the same time. He stared up at the little ripples of white cloud. They were going in to the State Library, to see what they could find out about The House of Records. 'I have a hunch,' Simon had said, 'we might find something out that would change things.'

'What sort of something?' David asked him on the train.

'I just wondered if it's really possible for them to know. Maybe they just guess. An informed guess, I mean. Use medical records, family history, general statistics on the population and so on. How could they be sure? How could they really know?'

'Medical records.' David swallowed an impulse to ask him how he was. After all, that would have been part of the reason Simon hadn't wanted him to know – not wanting to be pestered about how he felt.

'Lots of people think it's only a rumour about these records. But then we saw them, didn't we? It's not just a rumour.'

Simon's face was flushed. 'I wondered if it could be a hoax.'

'Keep your voice down. You're shouting.'

'Was I? Sorry. A sort of hoax or a punishment even, for breaking in.' (Now he was almost whispering, so that David had to lean forward to hear him.) 'For doing something that is outside permission. Do you see?'

'They wouldn't do that. That would be a terrible thing to do. Anyway, they didn't know we were there. Although . . .' He was starting to wonder about all those times he had felt he was being followed. Was it possible they *did* know, and that this was the result?

They walked up from the station in the sun and took the little path that snuggled in to the side of Government House. It was shaded and restful with creepers growing over the wall, and was another of David's safe places.

They found a computer in a quiet spot and did a search on The House of Records. Screenfuls of material flashed up.

Simon groaned. 'We'll never get through this lot in a morning.'

'There's two of us. There's no hurry. Pick out the most likely things first.'

Simon thought it might be a good idea to go through some of the material about its history: find out if it had kept widening the number and kinds of records it kept. David moved over to a nearby computer. He decided he would stick to articles about its function. They were more likely, he thought, to bring up material relevant to the records of termination.

But when he did locate them, most of the articles seemed timid, even censored. They amounted only to a list of facts about the institution and its use to the community as an efficient, centralising source of data.

He found that he was even starting to yawn as, over and over again, he read the same material couched in slightly different words. He was thinking of giving up and enticing Simon away for a cup of coffee, but decided to go back to the computer and run his eyes over the entire list of articles first. Nothing – although that *might* be something. He jotted down the word he didn't know. Minutes passed.

'Hey, Dave. I think we might be wasting our time. What about a walk up the street? I could do with some new sneakers – maybe. The camp really finished these.'

'Okay. I haven't found anything either.'

Thankfully they rushed outside and headed for the Mall.

Simon said, 'Did you see that girl as we came out, over by the old catalogue?'

'No.'

'She was looking at you as if she knew you.'

'What was she like?'

'Black hair. Tall.'

'Can't think who that'd be. Maybe she just fancies me.'

'Yeah. We're good-looking guys.'

'Guy. It was me she was looking at.'

They got the shoes in a sports shop near DJ's and searched for a café. 'That one'll do – over there,' said Simon, leading the way down Gawler Place. 'It's quietish and the food's good.'

They paid for their coffees and cake, and then sat at the window, on high, patterned stools. Simon had chosen an apple strudel and David, blackforest cake.

They munched away.

'I noticed how frantic you looked among those journals. Flashing over the pages, taking notes. Thanks.'

David flushed. He wasn't exactly disinterested. 'I guess I just like having you around.'

'And not underground.' Simon laughed.

'Something like that.' But David's mind was already filling up with unpleasant, wormy images. He shivered. 'There was a word I wanted to ask you about. He searched his pockets for the scrap

93

of paper. 'Here it is. "Prognosis". What's that mean?'

'You've asked the right one.' Simon's voice was wry. 'It means "prediction", I think. They use it medically. "The prognosis isn't good." Meaning you're likely to cark it. Have you been reading up on me?'

'No, it was in the title of an article.'

They looked at each other. Then simultaneously they leapt up, their stools wobbling horribly, and belted out of the shop, leaving the frothy bit of David's cappuccino behind.

They headed for their out-of-the-way computers, but these were already in use. They had to go to one in a more central, conspicuous part of the library.

'Here it is. *Prognosis. Latest Advances in The House of Records: The Efficacy of Prognostic Diagnosis.*'

They rushed to the journal section and started pulling the bound volumes off the shelf. But they were too old. The article they wanted was only from the year before. 'I'll go and ask,' said Simon.

'No, wait on. I'd rather we didn't have to. What about this box here?'

There was a solitary black box with loose editions of the journal inside it. David fumbled through the pile, but the number with the article in it was missing. He asked at the desk. The librarian scanned the computer. 'Ah,' she said, 'that's an article we keep on file. Just fill in this card and I'll get it for you.'

David stood on one leg and then on the other, filling in endless personal details. He wondered if this form would end up at The House of Records too.

Simon grabbed the article and rushed over to a seat in an alcove. He started reading, his legs crossed, head down. David recognised the pose of Simon-before-a-test. He hovered. 'Well?'

'It's all just about the other, boring sort of records so far – socio-economic status of various suburbs, belief structures thereof, graphs of hobbies, TV programmes watched, sleep patterns and so on – but it's leading up.'

'Then, skip. *Skip*!'

'It starts here.' Simon skimmed over the section. 'It says there's been a rumour for some time that The House also contains prognostic records. Then it talks about access to genetic charts, medical and hospital records, school and police material "and other sources of behaviour observation". I wonder what that means?'

'Secret service, maybe. Read the last bit.'

'It says it's long been known that it's medically possible to work out who is going to get which diseases, even down to the time of onset. It mentions Huntington's chorea as an early example, diabetes, Alzheimer's, propensity to cancer. Genes found related to alcoholism, depression.'

Over his shoulder David read the end of the article: 'Rumour will have it, then, that The House of Records does contain prognostic records relating to individual life expectancy. But these could surely only be approximate at best; nothing more, perhaps, than inspired guesswork. While we do not doubt the scientific basis on which these predictions are built, we must realise that they can be nothing more than predictions, however inspired. And the truth of the report has, of course, never been verified, least of all by The House of Records itself.'

'"Inspired guesswork",' said Simon. 'See, they don't really know, do they? There's that girl again. Over by the magazine rack. She's been listening to us.'

David looked up carefully.

'No. Over there.'

Puzzled, he considered the girl. Tall and striking-looking with black hair, dressed immaculately in shades of blue. He felt he'd seen her before, even thought he recognised the clothes. Perhaps she was one of last year's or the year's before, Year 12s. Familiar, yet unfamiliar at the same time. But when she started to move away, he could see who it was. The elegant, slow walk with the head held ever so slightly forward, was unmistakable.

'You should have gone up to her, asked who she was.' They were nearly home, walking back up from the station.

'I couldn't. And I didn't realise it was her, at first. Her real hair's auburn.'

'I guess it was still her real hair. It's just that she's dyed it. Or maybe she'd dyed it before.'

'Oh no.' David didn't like that idea. 'I'm sure she's a redhead. Her skin, her clothes, everything. What d'you think?'

'She's okay, I guess. I like them more like Susie.' He smiled as Susie, blond, uncomplicated, met them at the door.

'Am I glad to see you guys! I've just managed to get rid of Greg. I said you were coming on that train and we were going out.'

'What'd he want?'

'He wouldn't go away. Kept asking me to go to this thing at his work tonight. I said Mum wouldn't let me, but he kept on about it. And it's not even as though Cynth could come too . . .'

'Why not? Not that I think you should . . .'

'Cynth's sick. Glandular fever. I told you before, Dave.' She gave him a hug.

'Well, you're safe now,' said Simon. 'Come out with us instead.'

'That'd be nice.' Susie's face lost its worried look. She started to smile. 'It's just that he makes me feel uneasy. Unsure of myself. And he's always asking questions. About you, about Dave. Even about me. Weird sorts of questions.' She gave herself a little shake. 'Where are we going?'

'Somewhere really nice. We haven't worked it out yet. Somewhere for tea.'

chapter 20

SUSIE WAS DESCRIBING what had been happening at training. Or not happening. 'The swimming carnival's just over a week away and we're all getting worse and worse.'

'And fatter and fatter.'

'That too. But I'm still going to have soup *and* sweets as well as the main course. The soup looks so good. See, that table over there. It comes in one of those big tureens and they ladle it out. As much as you like.'

'Watch it,' said David. 'Two serves and you won't be able to eat anything else.'

'I'll eat everything. Even if I have to sit here all night.'

'Me too.' This was Simon. 'I'm starving. I've never had dinner this late. I'm having soup, chateaubriand for one and that toffee-looking dessert, whatever it is.'

They were sitting at a table right up against the cool slice of atrium that divided the room. It had been raining recently, and drops glistened on the dark green of the leaves. The cutlery was silver and the tablecloth pink with a white underlay. Waiters and waitresses hovered attentively around them. Susie had only stopped smiling briefly once since they had come in, when talking about her swimming. Now she was smiling around at everyone. 'I don't know how you're both affording this. Thanks, guys.'

'We've decided to spend up big,' said David, looking knowingly at Simon, who said, 'Not our usual kind of place, but it's quiet enough to talk here. Anyway, it's only the three of us and we didn't do anything for my birthday.'

'No. Why was that?'

'He was off-colour, remember?' said Susie. 'You look great, now.' She beamed. 'We were going to that Mexican place at North Adelaide and then on to the Piccadilly. There was that great film . . .'

David did remember, vaguely. Yes, it all fitted into place: Simon cancelling things at the last moment, being apparently unreliable, not like himself at all. He'd probably thought Simon was moving away, distancing himself, now that he went to a private school. What Simon was in at present, was it called 'remission'? Or was he better – really cured?

The waitress was hovering nearer. 'Two beers and a mineral water,' said Susie. She knew what the boys would want without asking. They sat quite still then, perusing the menu again with great solemnity. It wasn't often they went to a restaurant where there was a super choice like this.

'I feel like being sophisticated,' said David. 'I'm going for the Atlantic salmon.'

'I'll have the chicken breast stuffed with camembert. And we'll all have soup first.'

The soup was potato and leek, very smooth, very hot. It steamed invitingly on David's spoon and slid deliciously down his throat. He felt better, happier, at once. He would certainly have more.

'Taste the cream,' said Simon.

Susie was too busy to talk. She was attacking the warm wholemeal loaf that came with it. The crumbs scattered luxuriantly over the pink cloth. She looked up at last. 'I was just thinking today what I'll do when I leave school.' She paused, dramatically. David thought of all the things Susie had already (briefly) wanted to be: an editor ('Oh no!'); a teacher (even worse); a nurse, an astronomer. Whatever it was, he only wished he'd be around to see it.

'Well?'

'It's something where you're really needed, and people are always pleased to see you when you come.'

'A belly dancer,' suggested David.

Susie didn't bother to reply.

'A gardener?' (Simon.)

'Doctor.' But even as he said it, David knew it wasn't right. People wouldn't always be pleased to see you.

'House cleaner.'

'Plumber.'

'Getting closer.'

Silence.

'Give in? Archaeologist.'

'"Really needed"?' said David, through a mouthful of bread.

'"People always pleased"?' said Simon. 'What if you want to excavate their backyard, pull down their house?'

'History's important. If you don't know your own history, you don't know anything. You don't know how to act. People *should* be pleased. And I wouldn't disturb anyone.' She made her way, more slowly this time, through another bowlful of soup. 'You're still going to be a doctor, aren't you, Simon?'

Simon looked down at his bread. He buttered it carefully, end to end and then right round the edge of its thick crust. He looked up at David. An uncertain, a lost look.

'Tell us about Greg,' said David quickly, hoping to change the subject with a powerful topic. 'What weird questions did he ask?'

Susie flushed. 'It's not so much what he says, it's how he says it.' She frowned. 'And how he looks when he says it. He lounges up against the door and sort of leans over you. He's so big. Insinuating himself.' She shuddered. 'He's creepy.'

Simon looked reproachfully at David, as if to say, why get her upset? Simon could be so dumb sometimes.

'He just won't take "no" for an answer, that's what I can't stand. I say, "No, Greg, I won't go to the dinner, I won't go to the movie," and he keeps smiling on and on as if I've said "yes".'

'Keep on saying "no",' said Simon. 'It's sure to sink in at last. He can't have that thick a hide.'

David could see Simon was pleased, pleased that she didn't like Greg, glad that she found him 'creepy'.

'And everyone at school's been acting as if I'm going out with him. "Who's that dark hunk you're being seen with?" Jodie asked me yesterday. It's embarrassing.' Absent-mindedly, she picked up the last piece of bread. 'I suppose he *is* good-looking . . .'

Simon looked suddenly grim.

' . . . if you like that deep-featured style.'

David could see Simon relax again. Clearly Susie wasn't keen on 'deep features', whatever they might be. Something that Greg had, and he and Simon hadn't. 'Are we more the open-air look?'

'There you go, like Mum, relating it all to yourself. I'm talking about Greg, not you. But yes, I suppose so. You've both got more open faces; his is more closed in, secretive. He uses it to hide what he is, not to express it.' She munched on her bread with an air of triumph. 'Yes, that's it, of course. He makes me uneasy because his face doesn't show what he's really thinking. And I get the feeling there's something *behind* his asking me out. Like sometimes I can see he's *bored* being with me. I'm too young. But then, why does he bother? You two don't have that sort of guard up. I always know what you're thinking. Usually, anyway.' She sighed and looked up at David. 'At least when you were younger – like last year.' She laughed.

'To get back to you,' said Simon. 'I was a bit surprised. I thought you'd want a job more to do with people. Like a social worker or a vet.'

'I thought vets were to do with animals,' said David. But he was thinking Simon was right: you *would* expect her to choose work that was more to do with people. Yet there was something quirky, unexpected about Susie. He tried to formulate it to himself. She had *aspirations*, that was it. She might become *anything*, anything she set her sights on. She had more ambition, more drive, than he had. She would *become* something. The thought comforted him, as he knew, later, it would comfort his mother.

Simon was explaining. 'But you have to get through the people first, and there's often quite a complicated relationship between a pet and a person. You'd need to know a lot about people, and how to deal with them, to be a vet.'

'Almost a psychiatrist,' said Susie. 'Sounds too complicated for me. Digs are the thing. Objects. Things you can touch and identify and that don't change from minute to minute.'

Their main courses had arrived by now, arranged beautifully, appetisingly on white plates with an embossed edging, also in white. The vegetables came separately: duchess potatoes, tiny yellow squashes, bright green beans. David passed these around.

There was a contented silence. David was imagining Susie at her dig. It wouldn't be, but he imagined it as being somewhere like York in England. The grass was very green, and old stone houses huddled all around. Susie and her team were excavating around the foundations of a house that had had to be demolished. A wintry sun lit up her blond hair as it dipped in and out among the marked squares of the dig. Her face looked intent, serene. There was a park further over with trees almost bare. A few bright leaves still clung in among the twigs. The shape of the trees seemed noble, unveiled, not hiding anything. Trees with open faces.

His salmon seemed to have disappeared. 'Anyone want more veg?' he asked, then gratefully spooned the rest onto his plate.

'Fish isn't as filling as chicken,' said Susie. 'This is delicious.'

David could see the melted camembert flowing out of the pink-brown heart of the chicken. The fresh green of the beans with their cream sauce looked pleasant beside it.

'And not as filling as steak,' said Simon. His thick 'chateaubriand for one' could easily have fed them all.

They were really full, but were determined to order sweets. Susie was having fresh fruit, David profiteroles, and Simon the 'toffee thing' which turned out to be various berry icecreams with strawberries in a toffee and chocolate basket. They felt refreshed rather than heavier, after them. Later they sat, heads drooping sleepily over the steaming coffee, unwinding the wrappers of the accompanying chocolates. 'Wow!' said Susie. 'What a meal! Back to the drawing board, Mum.'

'Your mum's a lovely cook.'

David glanced around at the other people still left in the restaurant. Everyone seemed pleased, relaxed. He looked at the circle of contentment that was his own table. Susie was almost

101

purring. Simon had stretched his long legs right out into the space between the tables, and was smiling at something Susie had said. Suddenly he became aware of his happiness, and, at the same moment, he could see his mind frame the scene, take a snap of it like a photograph. He could feel the happiness change into something else. Something more aware. Something with just a hint of desolation around the edges of it.

chapter 21

DAVID TURNED UP the radio louder, to drown out anything that might be circling around in his head. Once, he had enjoyed his time in the car as a quiet space, without distractions. It was the following Monday and he was on his way to 'CanTeen'. Simon had asked him if he'd like to come, see what it was like. 'It's a kind of club.'

But David felt more and more anxious as he neared the city. He wouldn't belong in a kind of club. Simon was going straight in after school and he was meeting him there. He drove down King William Street and turned off by the cathedral. There was a parking station in the side street here, Simon had told him.

It wasn't the sort of parking station he'd have thought would have gone with a hospital. It seemed dark and inhospitable and had warning signs everywhere – implying bashings and robberies. 'Don't linger too long near your car' was the gist of them all. He was also unfamiliar with the set-up. You had to take a card from one machine and pay at another on the way out. There were no people involved at all.

He went in at the front entrance of the hospital and sat down uneasily to wait for Simon. The foyer was full of women and small children: children with bandages and crutches, children with white faces. His uneasiness increased. It seemed a grue-some idea, a hospital for children. As though it were a kind of tor-ture chamber. He'd been used to thinking of hospitals as places where you visited old people: people who'd had their stint. Not little kids like these. Five minutes. Ten minutes. Almost fifteen. He couldn't keep still. He'd have to get outside for a breath of air.

'Hey, where you off to?' It was Simon, grinning, looking a lot healthier than David felt. They fell into step, walking around the building and up the hill towards the back entrance to CanTeen. The light was turning pink from the late afternoon sun, but it only seemed to add to David's feeling of remoteness. 'Saves going through all the renovations. It's a bit of a mess at the moment.'

There were cranes and scaffolding everywhere: David could see it all now from the side. The building itself was a rich cream colour, its height softened by the parks around it. Petunias were still struggling to flower in the banks opposite.

'You sure I won't bug them?'

'No. It's mainly brothers and sisters but they won't mind you. It's nice to have someone to show it to. There mightn't be many here today,' he added, as they walked in and headed towards the lift. 'You never can tell.'

David felt his sense of unreality increase as they went up in the lift and came out at a narrow corridor. Several rooms branched off on one side. Noticeboards, some with newspaper clippings, lined the hallway. Simon stopped at the first room. 'This is ours.' He sounded proud, proprietorial. 'We can make coffee here, use the fridge, watch TV.'

David moved over to the window. The room looked out over the rest of the hospital and then over the city. Buildings rose, smokeless, to the greying sky. He turned round. The couches set in around the walls were a mustardy colour and the carpet a flat brown. It reminded David of Simon's old lounge room in Ethel Street. Maybe that was why Simon sounded so fond of it. There *was* no one around.

'It's early yet. Someone's sure to roll up. Come and meet Jim while we wait. He runs us.'

'Jim's' room was an even smaller one set in at the end of the passage. It was a bit brighter-looking with red armchairs and a large wood-grained desk with a dark-haired man, like part of the furniture, sitting behind it. He smiled up at David who was looking, but only vaguely, in his direction. Simon's words kept misting away, and David had to force himself to concentrate.

'. . . my best friend,' Simon was saying. 'Jim makes sure we don't need cheering up by keeping us killingly active.'

Jim rushed towards him. David noticed he was so much taller than Jim that he had to drop his arm down to shake hands. 'I've heard a lot about you, David. And that's not just a line. I'm really glad . . .'

'Simon has told you at last,' Simon completed for him. 'Actually it was detective work. He found out for himself.'

'Then he shouldn't have had to.' He turned to David. 'Maybe you'd come with us on our next camp – mid July. He checked the calendar. 'The 18th. Do come.' Startled, Simon and David looked at each other. The 18th of July . . .

Jim reached up and clapped Simon on the shoulder. 'And Simon's turning out to be one of our huge successes. How does he look, d'you think?'

'Great. He looks great.'

It was true. It was spooky, David thought. You wouldn't have believed there was anything wrong with him at all.

'You okay?' Simon asked him as they went back down the corridor. 'Come and have a cup of coffee.'

This time the room was filling up. There was a healthy, bouncy girl with two small boys on one couch ('Lisa and her brothers'), and a brown-eyed, enthusiastic-sounding boy with someone smaller and less noticeable on the other ('Gerald and Tom'). None of them looked ill. David stood, awkwardly sipping his coffee while the others talked about the last camp and a fun run they were going on. The claustrophobic feeling he had had in the foyer of the hospital started to return. He concentrated on his coffee and on the view out of the window. He was glad when another late rush of people surged in and he had to step outside.

He looked up at the newspaper clipping nearest to the lift. A sensible-looking boy, no older than themselves, stared out at him. He stood, for what seemed a long time, staring back. And then Simon was there, looking over his shoulder. 'Lisa's brother. Bit of a hero round here. Come in and meet Gerald. He's our president.'

Gerald seemed full of energy and drive, his brown eyes eager. He smiled quickly at David, but all his talk was for Simon. He spoke rapidly. Had Simon liked the venue for the last camp? Should they repeat it in July with a different group? Which parts of the programme should they alter? Had he thought any more about a guest speaker? David felt increasingly out of it, shuffling his feet uneasily as the conversation swung around to include Tom. Tom wanted to invite the president of the NSW branch, the branch which had recently completed a film about the families and lives of teenagers with cancer.

David could feel himself getting angry. He almost choked on his coffee.

Eventually Gerald turned to him. 'And what do *you* think about the camp?' The camp they wouldn't be around to see. Gerald sounded patronising, not really interested in what David thought.

David felt his frustration boil over. His voice came out louder than he intended. 'I think it's creepy, all this organising around death.' His hands shook around his mug.

His remark fell into a sudden silence. Gerald stared hard at him, then walked away. David wasn't sure from Simon's face if he'd heard.

He walked over to top up his coffee and wondered if he should talk to Lisa. 'Lisa's brother'. He had thought she seemed particularly happy, but now when he looked at her more closely, he could see it was not so. He tried to think of something to say to her. It might be risky to ask after her brother. But the moment passed and she turned away to talk to someone else. He was relieved when Simon touched him on the arm and led him out to the passage. 'Gerald's great,' he said, as they went down in the lift. He sounded tired. 'So enthusiastic. But he does go on rather. But what you said: it was a bit uncalled for, don't you think? What were you getting so wound up about?'

They walked down to the car park. David noticed he had to alter his pace, slower than on the way up. Simon was sounding so mature about it, hardly annoyed at all. A little sad, if anything. He felt himself getting angry again – at that, as well. 'He just seemed so . . . *pleased* with himself. And all that talk about a camp in *July*. When w . . . , when you . . .'

Simon put his hand on David's shoulder.

'And when I get mad, I don't seem able to hold it in.'

Simon sighed. 'What's new?'

'Is *he* sick? Gerald?'

'He's okay. It's his brother . . .'

'And Lisa's brother?'

'He died at Christmas time. It was a bit of a shock for them all. Usually, if you can keep going through the spring . . .'

'And they still hang around after . . .'

'It's amazing how it helps to be around people who understand.'

David felt himself turning hot. He wanted to scream at him, '*I* understand. I'm not an outsider.' Like Gerald talking on and on about the camp. How he'd felt about that: the bottom dropping out of the day, the space widening inside him. But he couldn't say anything, not yet. He would have to, though. He'd thought when Simon told him what was going on, the barrier between them would have disappeared. But it hadn't. Not altogether. And he was behaving badly – like today, with Simon's friends; like when he'd taken him rollerblading. Simon'd been *sick*, for Christ's sake. There were still blank spaces where he should have been talking to Simon, filling him in on how he too felt. 'It's worse for me. I'm not even ill,' he wanted to shout. 'Look at me. I can walk faster. I'm *healthy*.'

The car park seemed different now with Simon there, even though it was getting dark. They laughed at the warning signs and scraped the money together for the machine at the exit.

Simon seemed in reasonable spirits, in spite of everything. 'I always feel better when I've been, though I don't always want to go. Maybe I shouldn't have made you come. You've gone quiet.'

David hesitated. He'd been thinking about cancer, about it swarming everywhere up there. And especially, about it spreading, like a foul sticky grey jelly, inside Simon.

He gave himself a little shake. 'It's just hospitals. And like that – for kids. I've never been in a kids' hospital before. But I'm glad you took me.'

He couldn't explain, not yet, about how up in CanTeen he'd felt like a kind of ghost: a ghost that haunts streets and passageways where real people live. At one with the photos on the board.

He turned up the car radio so Simon wouldn't notice any more blank spaces, and steered him carefully through the traffic and the winking lights to his home. It was only after he'd driven off again that he noticed what had probably been happening for some time. He was being followed; this time he was sure he was. By the dark blue car with the roof-rack, the same car he'd thought might be following him that day on the Victor Harbor road.

He sped through the darkening streets. He wanted to head off home as quickly as possible, but knew that might be the wrong thing to do. If they saw him turn in, they would know where he lived; then nowhere was safe. Who could be so interested in him that they would follow him? Repeatedly. Unless it was one of those weird guys from The House of Records. He'd wondered about that before. Perhaps they were just keeping an eye on him, or . . . what if he was to get a delayed punishment for what he'd done? For doing what was not permitted. Perhaps they'd bring on his due date? But that seemed exaggerated, nightmarish, ridiculous. Maybe even paranoid. Could he be imagining it? He wove in and out of the streets that flanked Victoria Drive. The dark car followed at the same distance. Should he go back to Simon's?

107

Round another corner then back, a sly way, to the main road. He drove on, pleased with himself in the middle of his panic. He'd shaken them off yet again. Driving honours to him. But as he turned right, at Cross Road, there it was again. He accelerated up the narrow road and through the underpass; then swung right, instead of left, off Goodwood Road and this time wove in and out of the maze of streets opposite the showgrounds, still catching glimpses, but trying to ignore them.

Five more minutes of this, he told himself, then out onto Greenhill Road and home the long way. He raced down another winding street. It was dark, only dimly lit. He was almost at the bottom of it before he realised what he'd done: the street was a dead end. His eyes saw it before his mind could take it in. There wasn't time to reverse and go back. At the end of the road his headlights picked out the neat pattern of the driveways – like segments of an orange. He picked out one segment without cars in its drive, with no lights on that he could see. He cut his engine, turned the lights off, and freewheeled in, right round the side of the house. I'll say some blokes from school were chasing me, he thought, if anyone comes. He took his mum's slim car torch out of the glove box and sprang from the car. There was a thick rose-mary bush at the side of the drive. He crouched down beside it and waited. The rosemary was strong-smelling, almost pungent. It was a cool smell, but his whole body throbbed with heat.

The dark car cruised its way down. It faltered, as he had done, then slowly, at the end of the street, it turned around, its lights flashing over him. It stopped near the street light outside. David wanted to hide: hide under the car seat, run for the doorbell, shin up a tree. But he didn't. He forced himself to get up and look at the car. He was sick of being chased. He was sick of not knowing what was going on. In any case, you couldn't hide for ever.

There seemed to be only one person inside. He looked care-fully at the back seat. Empty. Then at the front again. There was something . . . almost familiar, about the driver. Something about the way . . . He edged down the drive, keeping to the shadow of

108

the trees. When he was almost sure, he shone the torch. A thin, clear beam fell across the car. He ran out onto the road, round to the driver's side. He flung open the door. 'So. It's you,' he said.

chapter 22

DAVID COULDN'T ANY longer put off telling Simon. It was Friday and he'd persuaded him to skip school. Not that Simon had needed much persuading. 'Sometimes I wonder why I bother going at all.' They were driving up to Cleland Wildlife Park, to one of David's 'safe places'. They'd got to the summit at Mount Lofty where the teashop had been before that last terrible bush-fire, and were taking the winding road down, past the ruined monastery.

David cleared his throat. Maybe it would be easier while they were still in the car, while he could still look out at the crumbling road ahead. 'There's something I've been wanting to tell you.' He could hear his voice wobble.

'About your dad?' Simon knew he always got upset when he heard from his father.

'In a way.'

He didn't often have fights with his mum, but when he did they were nearly always about his dad. He thought of their 'con-versation' that morning. His mother had been warning him against going to see his father: 'He always likes it to be on *his* terms. He maybe won't even *want* to see you.'

'Then I'll just turn up. I won't ring first.'

'Don't be ridiculous, David. He mightn't even *be* there. And what would you do for money? I don't even know what the fares are now. I haven't got that sort of money.'

'You don't have to have. I'll use the money for my car.'

109

'Your *car* money! But you've been saving up since you were twelve.'

His father had always been quite generous with money for birthdays, Christmas.

'Yeah, well. I've decided to spend it now.'

They drove into the car park at Cleland. The spaces for the cars were individual, made out of sleepers and arranged around where the trees were not.

'And?' prompted Simon.

'Dad wants me to go with him to Singapore later on in the year . . .' *Later in the year.* The words were like a bell tolling.

'You'll enjoy that.' Simon's voice was flat.

'But I'd rather go now.'

'To Singapore?'

'No. To see him in Sydney. Just for a weekend.'

They paid their entrance money and wandered into the park. They always started with the snake pit. They looked over its tiny wall, their eyes searching the tangle of undergrowth. The snakes, supposedly, couldn't scale walls. Susie would never go near. She said there always had to be the one that would learn how to climb, and a low wall like that must offer a lot of encouragement.

Simon wasn't saying anything. That was one of the nicest things about him; he would just wait for what *you* had to say. David tried to go on. 'Well, Mum's not keen on the idea and, of course, she can't see the point. And then there's the money . . .'

'D'you want a loan?'

'*No.*' He was horrified that Simon should think he wanted something of him. Well, he supposed he did, but certainly not that.

By now they'd passed the koalas and were standing by the lake. This must be one of the slowest conversations on record. In spite of himself and of what he was saying, David could feel the peace of the place settling on and around him. The little island, the gentle lake, the pelicans, the wild ducks paddling around. He'd even remembered the bread. He threw it to them in small,

110

manageable lumps. He thought it was here, at the lake, that the peace centred the most. Soon they would cross over the water to the aviary, and he would enjoy that too. Then they would walk through it to the sweeping enclosure behind, which housed different kinds of kangaroos. Then back by the dingoes' caves. But it was here that the peace centred. It was such a still day, not even the reeds moving, although, above them, small white clouds drifted across the blue sky.

'But there *is* a point, of course,' said Simon. 'Is it something to do with that girl?'

David was taken aback. 'What girl?'

'The one last week – in the library.'

'In a way.' Then, seeing the look on Simon's face, 'Oh nothing like that. But it *does* have something to do with the girl. D'you think she was following me around that day?'

Simon stared at him. 'More likely a coincidence.'

David knew he looked disappointed.

'What do you want me to say? That she's a spy or something?'

'Maybe.'

'Spying on you?'

David nodded, miserably.

'You've been watching too many movies. Although I must admit, I think I have too.' He sat down on a wooden bench.

A woman and two children were coming towards them, along the path that bordered the lake. One child was asleep in the pusher, the other seemed to be collecting bits of grass. The ducks waddled past them, unnoticed. David waited till they'd gone, then sat down beside Simon. 'What d'you mean?'

'I've had this funny feeling sometimes that I'm being followed. I told Jim, and he said it can be one of the results of being ill. You get a bit paranoid, think the whole world's against you, that kind of thing. F'r instance, I was in Rundle Mall yesterday, after school, and I caught this guy staring at me . . .'

David found he was arguing the other way. 'People do stare at one another. People are interested in other people.'

111

'But then he went straight off . . . And later I saw him again, in a bookshop. It just seemed odd.'

Talking about it had unsettled Simon. He headed off to the aviary with David tagging along behind. The double doors clanged behind them.

The Major Mitchell cockatoos were huddled up together close to the roof, but the sulphur-cresteds were more friendly. One came and sat on David's arm. He stroked it. Once, he would have been too frightened to do that. He could see there were advantages in not having so much to lose. He would go and visit his father, whatever his mother said. She would understand afterwards, or at least be glad that he'd gone.

But Simon had already clanged out of the other doors and was heading rapidly down the slope. Startled kangaroos hopped away on either side of him. David took a quick look round at the Port Lincoln parrots, the cockatiels and the musk lorikeets, deposited the sulphur-crested gently on a branch, and hurried after him.

Simon must be running. There was no sign of him at all. David decided he'd just walk. He'd find him soon enough. He strolled through the red gums with their resident kangaroos sprawled at the roots of them, and looked around – at the leaves, at the grass. Now he could see Simon: he was on his way back. He sat down and waited. 'You all right?'

'Sorry. Sometimes I feel I have to keep moving. I'm okay now.'

'Let's skip the dingoes. We'll go back to the kiosk, have some coffee. You can shout me a cake.'

He was still trying to tell him. Maybe face to face over coffee would be worse. Why was he finding it so hard? Perhaps it was because he believed, in a superstitious sort of way, that once he'd voiced it, that would make it come true. *Force* it to happen. Even more, saying it would also make him acknowledge it to himself.

They were nearly back at the koalas. He tried again. 'Sime, I know what you mean.' His hands were clenched, his whole body rigid.

'Mm?'

'About . . . keeping moving.' His voice came out tight, cracked.

'Thanks. But I don't think you could, really.'

If only Simon would give him an opening. He felt coiled up, inside.

They gazed at the koalas, more peaceful even than the ducks, asleep in their tree houses. Bright sunlight fell all around them on the grass.

'What I don't get, is how well I feel. It's getting nearer and nearer the time – and I feel better!'

There it was. The opening.

'Ever thought it could be an accident?'

Simon stared at him.

'Remember last week when you told me? I said, "You made me go with you." Didn't you think that was a strange thing to say?'

'Now that you mention it. What did it matter? What did it matter to you? We didn't get caught.'

'Then you said, about making me think your date was okay, "Wouldn't you have, if it'd been you?"'

Simon looked uncomprehending.

'It *was* me. It is me. It is me too.'

chapter 23

THEY SAT, SURROUNDED by tourist tea towels, sipping their coffee. At least, David was sipping his and eating his cake, wolfishly hungry now. Simon gazed, unfocused, at the wall.

'Want a bit? Carrot. It's very good.'

Simon shook his head. He looked up, his eyes distant. 'How could it be? How could it be you as well?'

'Why not? Car accident, perhaps.' He saw Simon shudder. 'Happens to lots of people. Lots of friends. You're more likely to be killed with a friend than with a stranger, just as you're more likely to be murdered by one.'

'But you've seemed much as usual. Although I suppose I've been so bloody caught up in myself . . .'

'Susie and Mum wouldn't agree – about me, I mean. Or about you, for that matter. But often, I just don't believe it.'

He was feeling light-hearted, almost exuberant, now that he'd told Simon. The tearoom was looking its normal self, the self he was used to, not stretched, not elongated, the way places had been looking recently. Like CanTeen. He would tell him about what had happened the other night.

But Simon spoke first. 'You couldn't predict an accident. *They* couldn't predict an accident. You couldn't do that, however many records you had. It wouldn't make sense. It would mean they could see into the future. It would make them God.'

'I don't know then. Maybe it's a coincidence, it being the same day. But I'm not even *ill*.'

Simon stared solidly at the tea towels.

David went on, 'You know how you thought someone was watching you, maybe even following you around – in the Mall, yesterday?'

He waited for Simon's eyes to lose their shocked, stunned look.

'When I dropped you off after CanTeen on Monday, someone was following me. Dark blue car with a roof-rack. Know it?'

Simon shook his head.

'And don't say I'm imagining it. I'd seen it before . . . It followed me down this dead-end road and I jumped out of the car and waited.'

'And?'

He'd got Simon's attention now.

'Guess who it was.'

'You mean we know this jerk?'

'Three guesses.'

'Greg.'

'What made you think of him?'

114

'Maybe he thought it was Susie in the car. Checking up on her. He's a bit weird, that guy.'

David smiled to himself. Simon was definitely jealous. No wonder; everybody cared about Susie. He had a flash of her standing in front of him in the lounge room, years before, when they'd been small. Their father had been in one of his black rages. He'd been ready to give David one of his savage psychological beltings. It was never physical, but David had often almost wished it were. He couldn't even remember now what it had been about. Something trivial, as usual. Susie had planted her feet out wide. 'It wasn't David.' Her voice was high and piping. 'It was me.'

His father's face had fallen: David had seen it fall, with rage in his own heart. His father wanted an excuse to vent his anger – and now he couldn't do it. He had never turned on Susie yet. She was too small, and yet too psychologically strong, to make a decent target. His father had slammed out of the house.

He looked up at Simon. 'Have another guess.'

'Someone from the hospital? Although I can't think why they would want to follow us home.'

'Nope.'

'Andrew and Tim.' (David's friends at school.)

David shook his head.

'I give up. Unless . . .' (here he grinned widely, making David think he'd just been teasing him by not mentioning her before), 'unless, of course, it was the girl.'

'It *was* the girl.'

'The girl with the false hair?'

'Not false hair. Just falsely coloured.'

Simon started to eat the crumbs from David's carrot cake, wetting his thumb to pick them up. 'What happened?'

David thought back to that night. To the way she'd looked up at him out of the car door. 'Hi,' she'd said, sounding quite cool about it. As if they'd met at the beach or the supermarket or something. 'You've caught me out. Just wondering where you live.'

115

'There, she fancies you,' said Simon, relaxing. 'She's just fol-lowing you around. Some girls are like that. Afraid of the direct approach.'

She'd ushered him into the car, kissed him gently on the cheek. She smelt of blossom. Then lightly on the mouth, then more insistently. She moved her head back and looked at him. His knees were turning to water. She kissed him again.

'Except,' he said, replying to Simon, 'I haven't told you where I met her first.' Or nearly first. He still had a niggling feeling he'd seen her somewhere before that. This girl, perhaps her, had been reading – or pretending to read. She'd been staring on and on at the cover of a book.

'Don't tell me,' said Simon heavily. 'This time I don't even have to guess.'

chapter 24

IT WAS THE next day. Saturday again.

'You wait here, Sue. I'll just pop in and see if he's home.'

As he opened the gate, David wondered why the Hatherleys' place always made him think of Hopkins. Stone walls, that was it. Enclosed by stone walls.

He knocked on the front door. It was Simon's mother who answered it. He could tell from her face that she knew, he knew, about Simon's illness. She said, 'It's nice to see you,' meaning it, her whole face lighting up, 'but Simon's gone off somewhere. I was out myself, so I'm not sure when he'll be back. Got time for a chat?'

'No. Sorry. Susie's waiting in the car. Can I see if he's left me a message?'

Since Simon had had a computer, the boys sometimes left mes-sages for one another on the screen saver. David switched the computer on, slipped in a disk, clicked on it and waited. Sure enough, there it was. *Back at twelve, Back at twelve*, made its way, at different levels, across the screen. David looked at his watch. 'Blast!' They couldn't wait that long with the kitten in the car. He turned to 'edit message' on the control panel and changed it to *Gone to Wingfield – kitten.*

He hadn't been in Simon's room for ages. Its window always gave an effect of freshness for it looked out on the dark green of the kidney-shaped pool. Yet the room itself was blue: dust blue carpet, blue-and-white wallpaper, slate blue curtains. It looked cool and ordered. Over by the window he noticed a red notebook lying open. He glanced at it. He could see Susie's name there, and after it his own. He looked more closely.

I still can't work out why he wanted me to take Susie. It was Susie he wanted me to take, not David. It doesn't make any sort of sense.

This must be Simon's journal. The doctor had told him it would be a good idea to keep one. Or perhaps it had been Jim, at CanTeen. He wasn't sure now. He peered at the writing and flicked back a page. He'd like to know who this mysterious 'he' was. Probably 'the guy'.

'David!' It was Simon's mother on the stairs. He turned the page over and hurried out, a bit flustered, onto the landing. 'Oh, there you are. Would you like some quinces for your mother?' She thrust a large paper bag into his hands. He thought how much nicer brown paper looked (and felt) than the more usual white plastic.

'Thanks, Mrs Hatherley. Mum'll be pleased.' He steered her quickly down the stairs and along the passage to the front door. It was a surprisingly hot day. Susie would be boiling, the kitten wilting.

'Why're we going this way?' Susie asked, as he drove back to Cross Road. 'Shouldn't we be heading more towards town?'

David grinned.

'Don't tell me.' She groaned theatrically. 'Petrol. You'd drive miles out of your way for cheap petrol. Poor, poor Peaches. She'll be worn out before we get there.'

David was glad, after all, it was just the two of them, although now that he knew about Simon (in fact knew more than Susie or anyone else did), he never minded when Susie said, as she always did, 'Can Simon come too?'

Even driving to Wingfield, the same route as to The House of Records, made David feel odd. They passed the bus he had caught that day: the day he'd met the girl, 'Andrea', for the first time. (He'd been right about the 'A'.) That night she'd told him her name, the torchlight picking out the fine bones of her face. He kept thinking about her, of her hands and her voice. *They* couldn't be faked. He wondered if he would ever see her again, long enough to find out which colour hair was truly hers.

The country grew flatter and drier; more desolate. There were no houses now, with their oases of garden. Only warehouses and indeterminate industrial complexes. Even the sky became greyer as they approached it. The air was so heavy now and foul they wound up the windows. It was a relief and a surprise when they drove up to the Animal Welfare cluster of buildings.

Trees and grevilleas, flowering red, greeted them as they swung into the narrow drive. Already the area smelt livelier, fresher. Almost, it could have been the entrance to a nursery.

'It *is* a nursery,' said Susie.

They identified the main building and carried Peaches in. There was no one sitting at the desk. Susie rang the bell. He wondered what they could do while they waited for the cat to be done and then for it to come round. It was far too far to go home and then come back. Sometimes there was too much time.

He wandered up and down the corridor and came back just in time to see Peaches being whisked away by efficient arms. Susie didn't even have time for a parting kiss. Before he could stop her, she was off, assuaging her worry by looking into the cages of all the cats and dogs, puppies and kittens, that were for sale. Staff were busily going around washing out the cages and bringing in some fresh batches of cats.

'I'm not sure this is a good idea,' said David, hurrying after her. 'In fact, I *am* sure it's a bad one.'

He shuddered as he looked at them. Being a kitten in here must be like living on death row. Spending your last days in a cage, without even the choice that he and Simon had about what they could do, where they would go.

Susie was hovering around one cage which housed a fluffy cream kitten with startlingly blue eyes. It had a little line of grey around its neck like a ruffle.

'Oh Dave, how sweet! Look at it.' The kitten was playing with the sleeves of the jumper that lined its bed.

'You can take it out if you like. Have a cuddle.' One of the workers was leaning on a broom, smiling at them.

'Don't, Susie.' David's voice was urgent. 'One kitten's enough. They cost a bit to run, you know.'

But Susie had already opened the cage and was lifting the kitten up gently. It nestled into the crook of her arm. 'And Cream,' she said, looking perfectly contented, her hair streaming out gold in the sunlight. 'Peaches and Cream.'

'What do you want to do while we wait?' he asked, hoping to distract her. 'We could go into town, although it's a bit of a trot . . .'

'Even on cheap petrol . . . What else is around here?' Reluctantly, she detached the kitten and poured it back onto its jumper. They strolled over to the car. A pincushion tree hung over them in pink. 'What's that?' She pointed over the roof of the hospital section. An enormous grey building, forbidding-looking even from here, towered up against the lighter grey of the sky. 'Maybe we could go there.'

David shivered as he looked at it. 'Come on,' he said. 'We're going to town.'

chapter 25

WEDNESDAY. SUSIE'S AUTUMN swimming carnival had finally arrived. It was being held at an inside pool only a few streets away, and Susie had been darting in and out to watch the trucks arrive with extra benches, to see the balloons and banners going up and the little red flags stretched across near the end of the lanes. 'It helps get me in the mood,' she said. Six local schools were competing, including two private ones, and Susie was anxious to swim at her best. 'I should have been more careful with my diet; I should have trained more,' she was moaning again.

The carnival was due to begin at 7 pm, and Susie and her mum and David were there by 6.30. David paced around outside the pool area, waiting for Simon. He was having one of those days where he couldn't keep still, where he felt the time he had left was simply washing away like the water at the beach.

But 7 o'clock came and nothing happened. There seemed to be umpteen delays and difficulties: the worst was that one of the schools seemed to have forgotten to turn up, or had mistaken the time. David had an absurd desire to rip out the lines of little red flags and run with them from the pool.

'Hi,' said Simon. 'Oh good, they haven't started yet.'

The place was packed with teenage girls. Those still in tracksuits were beginning to strip them off. 'Wow!' said Simon. 'What a show! There's Susie over there, slapping her arms around.'

'She's warming herself up. She always does that.'

They moved in and out of the crowds around the pool side, eyeing off the girls. 'Name your top three,' said Simon.

David looked around him, in a more concentrated way this time. Picking out girls was a serious business, or had been, in the past. It was harder to tell with the ones who wore caps. They might be stunning, but usually they didn't look it. Half-heartedly he picked out a dark Italian girl, a blond with long legs, and a girl who, though in a cap, still managed to seem pretty good. He pointed them out, without any great enthusiasm, to Simon, wondering at the same time how Andrea would look in swimming gear.

'So they don't rate with the spy with the changing hair?'

David looked at him. It was true what Simon said. He wasn't certain he trusted Andrea, but she sure spoiled him for anyone else. Not that there was much point now. Unless, just to see . . . 'What about you?' he countered. 'Which are yours?'

Simon smiled. 'Me? Oh, I only have eyes for Susie.'

His tone was light, mocking, but David thought there was an undertone of sadness in it too. And he was sure he meant it, whatever the tone. He followed Simon's eyes: he was certainly staring at her now.

'Doesn't she look . . . ?'

But Simon didn't say how Susie looked. She was over by the blocks, pulling on her cap. Invincible, David thought: *that* was how she looked.

They went right up the back, 'to get a girloramic view' as Simon put it. David could see his mother sitting with some of her friends in the very front row. And now he could see the late school rushing in through the turnstiles, squealing and shouting.

Tension had built up around the pool just before 7, but then collapsed as they waited. Now it was building up again. Susie was jogging up and down, trying to keep herself from seizing up. Her event was second on the programme.

The 100 metres seemed to be almost over before it started. David had been having another look at the blond with the long legs and nearly missed it altogether. Jodie (a friend of Susie's) came second. But the school was expecting to win the 200. It was expecting Susie to win.

David forced himself to keep still as the girls positioned themselves on the blocks. *Crack*, and they were away, all hitting the water together. David could hear Simon's sharp intake of breath. Susie's start looked good, her clean, graceful dive taking her well

121

up the pool. Usually she kept close to the leaders and then turned it on for the last fifty metres. Third at the turn, and racing back to the halfway mark. Her style looked smooth, controlled. She was swimming well. Up to the hundred-and-fifty and *second* at the turn. It was almost a foregone conclusion. Now she would put on her characteristic mesmerising burst of speed. David sat back to enjoy it. She'd hit the front by a fingertip. Twenty-five metres to go. But surely . . . Yes . . . Susie was fading! It wasn't that the others were going faster; her stroke was slowing right down. A moan from Simon. David's stomach muscles tensed up as he tried to will her faster through the water. She touched the side a fraction after David's blond. Cries of anguish went up from her team.

'Aw, she must have had a stitch,' said Simon. 'Poor Susie, she'll be so upset. Blast and damnation. I thought she had it in the bag.'

'I wish we could talk to her now.' David felt almost unbelievably disappointed. Cheated. All his excitement draining away. But then these days all his reactions were exaggerated. It was only a race, after all. But it would have been something: something to etch into the bland face of time, Susie, winning her race.

Afterwards she just said, shaking it off, 'No. I didn't get a stitch, though thanks for thinking it, folks. I got so out of breath you wouldn't believe. In fact, I still am, a bit. I must be so unfit.'

chapter 26

'YOU MEAN YOU booked a seat! You just booked a seat without telling me? And now you're too sick to go!'

It was Friday evening and David was sitting groggily on the side of the bed, trying to pull on a sock. 'I *am* going.' The room spun around. Susie hovered in the doorway. 'I have to go. I'll be fine once I'm on the plane.'

'David. You've got the flu. It's raging all around. You know it's the flu. You can't go. Now what are we going to do about this ticket?'

'What kind is it?' asked Susie, edging in.

David put his head in his hands. 'The cheapest I could get.'

'Insurance?'

'No, I didn't bother. It was another fifteen dollars.'

Everyone groaned.

'Then Susie will have to go. Your dad would be too disappointed, and we're not wasting a good ticket. In any case it never made sense – you'll be seeing him in December. It's more sensible if Susie goes. It's all working out for the best.'

'It isn't bloody working out for the best!' He'd hoped for so much from this trip: that he and his dad might finally like each other, not just pretend to, off and on. It might be their last chance. 'It doesn't make more sense. It's me who has to go. I *am* going.' He was shouting, the nearest he could get to it. He reached into the wardrobe for his jacket, his head pounding, his eyes like lead, a thick feeling of exhaustion in the pit of his stomach.

They watched him totter around like a demented fly, then Susie pushed him gently onto the bed.

'Susie can't go!' He was almost crying. The words came out as a whimper. 'They're not just non-refundable, the tickets, they're non-everything. Non-interchangeable too. You can't give them to somebody else.'

'No one will notice.'

'She's a girl, for Christ's sake.'

'I'll wear your parka. Shove my hair under a cap. That'll have to do.'

He could see Susie was starting to enjoy herself: she loved the unexpected. And Cynthia was still too weak to do much at weekends. Susie'd been a bit stuck, lately. He listened bitterly, as she flew in and out of rooms. So much for his attempt to tie up ends. So much for his attempt to do the right thing. He turned his face away, sweating and shaking, just stopping himself from wishing he were dead.

The door slammed, the taxi drove off, the house lay still. He hadn't realised what a difference it would make with Susie not there. The house had gone hushed, waiting; then desolate. He hoped he would never have to live here without her. Of course, she'd been away that time before – with Simon, but he hadn't been stuck in the silent house, listening to it.

David tried to read, but the small print of the Stephen King hurt his eyes. The day washed by. He dozed, he dreamed. They were playing *Nightmare*, he and Simon and Susie. Simon's greatest fear was still of long, clean corridors, stretching endlessly away. Susie's was of fire, and his of suffocation by water: grey, murky, shifting. And then he seemed to be in the car, driving down towards Largs Bay. His father had often taken him there, to see the house where he (his father) had been born. He'd chosen the Military Road, which should have taken him straight there, but the road kept disappearing into a serious of intersections and dead ends. He retreated back to Seaview Road and drove along it. And there at last was the Largs Pier, shining brightly in the sunshine.

He was walking down the jetty, the sea, jewel-green below him. The wind blew through his hair, his shirt. He turned round, looking for someone. There should be someone here, someone beside him. He felt empty, desolate. The wind roared in his ears.

'Susie rang. Oh, only for a minute. I was so relieved. I couldn't get through to your father. "Everything's fine," she said.'

David tried to sit up. 'And that was all? That was all she said?'

'Your father's phone, David. You know what he's like.'

It wasn't like Susie to say very little, even long distance, even on his father's phone. He was sure there must be something wrong and then worried that it was just him, seeing everything in the same drab way.

'Oh, and somebody else rang. Someone called . . . Anthea? No, Andrea. Said she'd ring again.'

'*Andrea* rang? Are you sure?' What on earth could she want? Tailing him, frightening him to death. Then kissing him. He hadn't told Simon about *that*.

His dream was coming back to him. She'd said she lived at Largs. Perhaps that was why he'd dreamt it. Was it Andrea who should have been there with him?

'Mum. What's the date?'

'The 15th, I think. Yes, of course. The 15th of May.'

And at her answer, he turned his face slowly to the wall. There were so few days left.

It wasn't till the next day that his mum produced a manuscript. 'I don't want you to read it,' she explained. 'I thought maybe I could read it to you.'

David groaned. In a way, he just wanted to lie still, worrying. Or not really so still. He'd tossed and turned so much that the sheet under him felt like the ridges of sand at the Largs Pier. I've gone off fiction.'

'I know what you mean. It would be quite restful to edit some factual material for a change. Just check up on facts, iron out the prose. Fiction writers are always much more sensitive about their words, their style . . .'

'Especially when they haven't got one.'

But his mother had started to read. The words flowed over him, falling in little streams and eddies around him. His mother's voice was soothing, musical. No wonder he and Susie had always enjoyed being read to. You wouldn't believe it – all this and the flu too, and he wouldn't be able to see Simon during the week. It was the first thing his mother had thought of: the importance of Simon not catching it.

'Well?'

'That was lovely.' He smiled, vacantly, at her.

'*Lovely?*'

'It sounded nice, anyway.'

'Mm.' His mother flicked through the manuscript again. 'She

does have a sense of rhythm, this writer, but the story didn't seem to have much plot.'

'Like life.'

'I've never really been sure about that myself. Surely one's character must give a bit of plot to one's life. You know, making the same mistakes, over and over. Falling into the same problems with relationships.'

Maybe he *could* ask her, after all. Talk to her about it, but in a sort of disguised way.

His voice came out hesitant, embarrassed. 'What about endings? Do endings alter the plot?'

'Mm. That's interesting. I suppose once writers know how their story is to end, they'd have to go back over the earlier bits and put in pointers to it. Yes. Yes of course, that *is* what they do.'

'But in real life you don't know what the end is.'

'Not usually; although I suppose at some stage you must have a fair idea, especially as you get older. You've *had* the pointers, the signs.'

Yet he and Simon weren't older. He blurted it out: 'Mum, if you knew you were going to die, what would you do?'

His mother stared at him. He'd perhaps made it sound more intense than he'd wanted to. He was even sitting up, leaning his elbow on the pillow.

'It's just the flu, David. The flu always makes people depressed. It happens to everyone. And I'm sure Simon . . .'

'No. I mean, there's this guy, and he *knows* he's going to die. What should he do?'

'Can he run away from it?' asked his mother, carefully.

'Not really. Because he doesn't know what form it's going to take.'

'Oh, I see.' She sounded relieved. 'It's a story you've been reading.' She picked up the Stephen King.

chapter 21

DAVID LOOKED AT his watch. Sunday, May 24. He could understand why Simon didn't wear his any longer. He'd explained how much time he'd spent at the hospital looking at clocks. They were all very round and bland, encased in stainless steel. But what he noticed most were the prominent red second hands. The same clocks were in all the waiting rooms, radiotherapy theatres and even in the tiny examination rooms, over the bed. The clocks, Simon said, show you, on the one hand, how precious time is; on the other, they show you time dribbling away. He'd spent hours waiting around in the hospital, staring into the fish tank at the unlikely coral: plastic, and gaudily painted in pink and blue and green.

David, on the other hand, had become obsessed with his watch. As the days on the calendar peeled steadily away, he could hardly bear to waste the time: waiting for people, waiting in queues. A woman in the butcher's had taken his place and he'd been flooded by sudden rage. 'It's *my* turn,' he said, shouldering her out of the way. He felt furious and knew he looked furious as he glared at her, ignoring her look of shock. And now he was waiting for the girl. Where on earth was she? He paced up and down the hall.

'Dave? I haven't told you properly about Dad. All the details. Mum's always been around. Come into the lounge?'

He sat down ungraciously on the old couch. It wheezed and groaned as he shifted around.

'When I got there, he didn't even answer the door. I thought, I'm in Sydney with forty dollars and nowhere to stay.'

'He *was* in?'

'Oh yes. But phased out in some way. He didn't even seem to know who I was. Just stood looking at me as though I was the Avon lady.'

127

'The devil drink.'

'I don't think so. He didn't smell of anything. Or nothing like that. I felt uncomfortable the whole time.'

'It was me who was supposed to be going.'

'What d'you think's wrong with him?'

David thought about how he'd been feeling himself recently: irritability and the desire for sudden action alternating with periods where he felt he'd fallen into some huge pit. 'Depression, probably. He's no good with people and he's no good on his own.'

'And why wasn't he expecting me? Or you, rather?'

'Didn't know I was coming. I thought if I wrote, he'd put me off, and he wasn't in when I rang. Or didn't answer the phone, more likely.'

'And you bought a ticket anyway? With some of your car money. What's all the urgency? Did you have a premonition or what?'

'You could call it that,' said David bitterly, 'if you wanted to.'

'I don't want to. I want to know what's going on. Look, Dave, Simon's going to be okay. Just because he's been so sick it doesn't mean . . .'

But it was so much worse than that. David couldn't bear to sit a moment longer. Besides, he thought he heard the gate click. He moved over to a window.

'Who on earth is that?' asked Susie, as a tall, expensively dressed, beautifully groomed girl walked up their narrow drive.

Andrea was heading towards the sea, he realised. Her hands were pianist's hands, slim and fine upon the wheel. She kept lifting her fingers up and down as she talked, and even turned to face him. The worst kind of driver. He snuggled into his seat belt and braced his feet against the floor. They were turning onto Tapley's Hill Road, driving, in the autumn sunshine, towards the airport. But she turned off at Africaine Terrace and drove up to the beach road. 'A bit of sea air. Just the thing for post-flu blues.'

'How did you get my number? My address?'

She said, in a spy-like voice, 'Ve haf vays of finding out zese sings,' then laughed and dispelled the impression. 'Well, I did know your registration number . . .'

He would find it hard to say, but he would say it in any case. Her hair was auburn today, the colour he thought was her own, and her eyes the grey-brown that seemed to go with it. She was dressed immaculately in shades of burnt orange and cream. Like an autumn leaf herself. 'What is it you're after?'

She turned and looked at him, both hands momentarily off the wheel. Maybe this was how the accident would happen. (But if an accident were predicted, you couldn't call it an accident, could you?) She laughed, her whole face softening. 'What could I be after but you? Aren't you used to being chased?' She touched his cheek with one of those flying hands. 'You should be.'

The sea air was blowing on him through both windows, the light was mellow and kind, not harsh and white as it was in summer. He had this beautiful girl, suggesting she was crazy about him, by his side. Then why did he feel wary, anxious, disbelieving, tracked down? He would like to believe. He thought of Simon's words, about illness. 'Illness can make you paranoid,' Jim had said. 'Just keep it in mind.' He would, but not too strongly. He had met her first at The House of Records.

They were driving now up Seaview Road – through Henley and Grange, past Ozone Terrace, a street he could remember from his dream. He'd gone down Seaview Road and turned into Ozone, only to find that Military Road was blocked off, yet again. He shivered a little. 'Where're we heading?'

'Wait and see.' She smiled at him, leaning her body ever so slightly towards him. Off Seaview Road and up to the sea front. The long straight stretches of beach that released the heart so that it soared like the seagulls up to the throbbing blue of the sky. It must still be the flu, he thought. I'm getting delirious.

'What d'you usually do on the weekend? Got a best mate?'

'Simon,' he said, without thinking. 'We usually hang around together.'

'Simon . . . ?'

Again without thinking, 'Hatherley. Why?'

The huge solid arched form of the Largs Pier Hotel was looming up, its jetty stretching right out into the sea. Once ships had docked here and steam trains run.

She was actually pulling up. Stopping.

'Why here?'

'Why not?' She swung herself out of the car in one easy movement. David lumbered along behind her. 'Obligatory icecream at the kiosk,' she said, 'then walk along jetty.'

She had chosen only vanilla, and just toyed with it. She passed it to him.

He stumbled in the thick sunshine, feeling clumsy beside her, licking on the cones alternately. The sea rose up deep green beneath them. She slipped her arm through his.

'Obligatory walk on the sand,' he said later, taking off his shoes and running down onto the flat. He slowed at the water's edge, waiting for her to catch up. He turned back and looked for her. She was wearing high heels and stockings – he hadn't thought of that. Not standard beach wear. Not how he'd imagined her at Susie's carnival. Now she'd stopped, was taking off her shoes. She laughed as she ran through the sand, still in her stockings, towards him. She stumbled as she reached him and he held out his hand for her. He felt almost happy, normal, as they trudged along while dogs ('under reasonable control'?) scampered past and seagulls flew over them. Families were arriving with buckets and spades to make the best of what might well be the last warm spell.

'Do you go to the beach much? You and Simon?'

He felt a prickle of unease. Why was she so interested in Simon? Could it be Simon she was really interested in? Or was he just being paranoid again?

'Sometimes. Me and Susie more. We go to Brighton.'

She had turned him around now, back in the direction of the jetty, back in the direction of the car. The feeling of his dream came back to him, the dream he had had that night with the flu.

He had woken with tears in his eyes. He'd been looking for someone. Someone on the jetty. Had it been Andrea? But even as he
thought it, he knew it wasn't so. The someone he had been looking for, the someone who should have been there, was Sue.

part THREE

'What will happen now?'

'We'll have to see.'

'But if Simon doesn't know . . . ?'

'He can still choose. It's up to him to choose.'

'And David?'

'You're still interested in him?'

'Will David at least be all right?'

'We'll have to see.'

'And Simon? Simon Hatherley?'

chapter 28

HE FOLDED HIMSELF into her car. She took off before he'd even properly shut the door. He did up his seat belt hastily. 'Hey, what's the rush?'

She'd been glancing at her watch. 'Didn't realise it was this late. And there's something I want to show you.'

She shot down the main street (such as it was) of Largs Bay. Nice though, sleepy. A café, a second-hand bookshop, antiques, old furniture. He wouldn't have minded having a browse around. He looked at Andrea. She was sweeping her long hair back behind her ears with the sensitive hands he kept noticing. Her ears were small and neat, well worth tucking her hair back to show. Across the railway line and an abrupt turn left. She pulled up outside what looked like a tiny colonial cottage: single-fronted with old red bricks out of white grouting and an equally old-looking, small, side verandah. Leadlight windows. She sprang out of the car. 'We're here.'

'And where's that?' David followed her up the brick path leading to the front door, tucked in at the side of the house. The door had leadlight in it too.

'Home. Where I live.' She pulled out her key and let him in.

The narrow room was filled with the golden light of afternoon. The walls were high and painted a maize colour with a frieze of flowers just below the ceiling. The doors and frames were wood, unpainted. A chaise longue took up one corner and there were two small (what looked like Edwardian) chairs upholstered in red along one wall. But Andrea flung herself into a modern, relaxed-looking sofa at the end of the room. She patted the place next to her. 'We've got it all to ourselves.'

He looked at her, uneasy, and sat down on the edge. The room had a pleasant feel to it; he liked it. Old, but with money enough around to make it comfortable, even elegant. He said as much, at least about its atmosphere.

Andrea seemed to respond to that. She bounced up again, losing the faintly bored look he had seen falling over her face. 'Have a look around. We've expanded it a bit.'

'We?'

'Me and my dad.'

So the gorgeous creature lived at home. He was surprised.

Proudly, she showed him the extensions to the house. A new kitchen and family room had been built on at the back, and a huge attic room above. It was done out in pine: pine floorboards, natural-finish pine furniture. 'It was going to be mine, up here, but my dad liked it so much he stole it. It's his study plus guest room, I suppose. Still, I like it below.'

She seemed fidgety, almost nervous. Not as he'd seen her before. 'Coffee?'

'Thanks.' He was feeling more at ease, now that she seemed less so. He saw her glance again at her watch. 'But if you've to be somewhere else . . .'

She smiled and shook her head.

He prowled around the family room, waiting. One wall was made of glass. She didn't seem like any of the girls at school. But then, if you saw someone in their own house, it made you feel differently about them. He sat down, finally, on a cane lounge that looked out on the garden, all lawn and shady big trees. A miniature version of Simon's.

She handed him a mug of steaming coffee and a saucer piled high with biscuits: chocolate one side, plain the other. He chewed away, watching her. She'd sat down on a cane chair opposite, not eating, not drinking. Just looking at him. Halfway through his third biscuit she took his mug away, put it deliberately on the coffee table in front of them and sat down again, beside him. She kissed him on the cheek, then on the forehead, leaning her body into him. He felt himself grow hot and tense, yet, at the same time, he had the oddest feeling that it was all play-acting, re-enacting a scene in a film or even from a TV commercial. He reached out and kissed her on the mouth. Let's see, then.

138

She responded straight off. It must be true, he thought in a befuddled sort of a way. Simon was right. She *was* crazy about him. That's why she kept following him around. Now she was letting herself fall back, almost lying on the couch. He kept kissing her, pressing her down. Gradually he moved his hand away from her arm. He had marked the flesh where he'd pressed it. Let his hand lie lightly over the soft material of her blouse. He could feel the curve of her breasts rising through it. He was breathing faster. So fast, as if he'd done fifty laps of the pool. He felt hungry. *Lonely.* He pressed his body in, right over hers, and kissed her more slowly, deeply.

That's when she wriggled; that's when she pulled away. So much for that, he thought, feeling irritated, *angry*, with her again. But wait. What was this? She was taking his hand, was leading him out to the passage, into the bedroom that branched off from what must be her study. He half noticed a family picture on the desk.

He followed her in. He felt . . . grateful. She was sitting on a very low, wide bed, unbuttoning her blouse. He watched as it slowly loosened, unable to believe his luck. Her breasts rose out from it. So white, shaped like pears – smooth, swollen, ripe. She was beautiful. He held himself still, in the doorway, just for a moment, savouring it, staring at them.

He walked towards her, his eyes shifting upwards to her face. He couldn't believe it. She looked bored, stony-faced, as if she were just managing to suppress a yawn. It made him think again about Greg, about Susie saying he seemed bored when he was with her. 'He thinks I'm too young.' He drew back, stood in the archway staring carefully, and only, at her face. 'What is it?' he said at last. 'What is it you want with me?'

She was holding on to both his hands, was pulling him down on the bed. Now she was opening his shirt, was caressing him through it, her face hidden. But all he could see was that expression in her eyes. Yet why not make use of her, the way she seemed to be making use of him? Experience it. See what it was like, while he had the chance.

139

Her hands still moved over him, yet he held himself rigid. She was kissing his chest, spreading his shirt out wide with her hands. 'David, Dave,' she said into it. Suddenly he got up, pushing her over on the bed as he did so. He felt bitter. Contemptuous. He tucked in his shirt. She stared up at him, puzzled. Not upset. Puzzled.

'Next time, pick up a fellow robot,' he said as he banged his way out of her room, slammed his way out of her house.

He heard her calling as he crossed the sun-drenched road and headed up to the station. It was going to be a heck of a long way back.

chapter 29

HOT, EXHAUSTED, FURIOUS he banged open the gate, walked up the path. Simon was in the lounge, talking to Susie. He got the feeling they might have been holding hands. 'Tell us. Susie says you've been out with a real looker. Dark horse! Someone from school?'

David looked over at Susie, then just the tiniest glance at the door. She picked up the hint at once, and left. You could always trust Susie not to pry, not to listen in on what he didn't want her to know.

'So, The House of Records girl.'

David's mind went back to the station. He'd walked up onto the platform feeling light-headed and odd and sat down in the iron shelter. He'd looked around him, felt as if he were in some sort of surrealist landscape. He'd pulled out his wallet to see if he were going to have enough for the train when it should eventually come, 'and that's when I saw it. This white car drove past me, drove down their street. Of course, it was all very quick, but I'm

140

sure it was her father. It was quite a small, little-used sort of a street. And there was a photo on her desk . . .'

'Well, that explains the hurry. She didn't want to be caught by her dad.'

'No. You're right. But that's not what I meant. Oh blast, here's Mum.'

David's mother dropped her rucksack at the door. 'Hello, Simon. Am I ever beat! We've just walked from one end of the National Park to the other. Or that's how it seemed. Come and talk to me while I get the tea on.'

David glared at her. '*I'm* talking to Simon.'

'Then that means it's my turn now. Simon, I haven't seen you, with David being sick. He still seems pretty crabby, but how d'you think he looks?'

Simon followed the flow of talk into the kitchen, leaving David, ready to kick anything in sight, alone in the lounge. Susie bounced in. 'She's terrific-looking, Dave. Is she nice too?'

'I'm not sure.'

She sat down beside him. 'That's how I feel about Greg. Only worse. In fact, I'm sure he's *not* nice. You know, something happened just before I went away.'

'Oh?'

'Yes. He was waiting for me after school.'

'Waiting for you?'

'In the car. With a couple of his mates. He wanted to take me home, but the others all looked pretty rough. And as if they'd been drinking.'

'So what happened?'

'I said I was meeting you.'

'And then?'

'They followed me up the road. In the car. Tooting. "Where're you meeting Dave?" Greg kept saying. "By this tree, that tree?" I felt stupid.'

'He needs sorting out.' He clenched his fists, ready. 'What a jerk.'

'That's what I thought. But then, he's Cynth's brother.'

'That doesn't mean anything.'

'Don't tell Mum, though. She'd only worry. They were probably only having a bit of fun.'

She switched on the TV. David sat dazed in front of it, his mind full of unpleasant images: the deserted station, bleached with sunlight; Greg playing games with his sister; the dark bedroom with Andrea . . . Now the news was coming on. He watched dully as hordes of people far away slaughtered one another. It made you wonder: what did it matter – one life more or less? He tried to rouse himself. Take an interest in somebody else. He turned to Susie.

'Tell me. Where did you go with Dad when he came out of his stupor?'

'Nowhere much. Into town, over to Manly, on the monorail, Darling Harbour.'

'Sounds all right to me.'

'It was, really. I suppose it's just he didn't have much to say. And when I talked, he didn't listen. Except once.'

'Go on.'

'I was saying something about going somewhere with you in the car. And he said, "Is David driving already? I'd rather he didn't." He said to be sure to tell you that at your age, you can't be careful enough. He kept saying it.'

'Did you tell him about Simon?'

'What about Simon?' said Simon. 'Dinner's ready, folks. Made partly with my fair hands.'

Susie inspected them, and he bowed, took her arm and led her in to dinner. David followed, more slowly.

On the day, he wouldn't drive. At least he could do that much for his father. He would say to Simon that he mustn't either. They would stay at home, perhaps separately, perhaps together. On no account must they go out in the car.

142

chapter 30

FIFTEEN DAYS. SIMON and David walked out on the Brighton jetty. The planks felt rough and uneven beneath their feet, and squeaked a lot. Through the widish spaces they could glimpse the sea. There were some crumpled-looking old men up the end, fishing. One of them was reeling something in. David leaned over the rail and watched. Now he could see the silver of the fish rising up through the clear green water. He shivered a little. That was how he felt, he thought, looking away: like a fish caught on a hook.

Simon asked, as they strolled back, 'What were you telling me last Saturday, about the girl's dad?'

'You'd say I was paranoid, like Jim said.'

'Maybe, but probably not.'

'I thought I recognised him.'

'Don't tell me. It could only have been from . . .'

'The House of Records,' they said together.

'I know it seems a bit much. But I'm sure he was. Fact is, I think it was that man on the 28th floor.'

'Could be. They do have families, you know. Heard from her again?'

'Mm. A letter this time.' David stopped at the shore end of the jetty, looked out to sea.

It had been a strange little letter:

Dear David,

Give me another chance. It is in your interest *to give me another chance. I'm coming for tea next Sunday night. About six.*

Yours,

Andrea.

'You mean tomorrow?'

David nodded. 'Nobody invites themselves to tea like that, do they?'

'Unless they want to meet the rest of the family.'

'I've only been out with her once.'

'What you going to do about it?'

'Nothing I *can* do. I don't know her phone number and, only vaguely, her address. Not even her last name.'

'She's certainly got plenty of nerve. Can I come too?'

'Of course.' David thought about it. 'She did ask something about you. I can't remember what, now. Perhaps I mentioned that you come for tea Sunday nights. Hey, maybe it's *you* she wants to meet.'

'Why not? I'm a good-looking guy. But you might be right. Maybe she's trying to kill two birds . . .'

It was such a cliché, yet David felt himself shiver at it. He changed the subject. 'What's happened to CanTeen these weekends? You never seem to be going anywhere with them.'

'Just seems a waste of time,' he said, as he swung down onto the sand. 'I'd rather be with you.'

'And Susie,' David added, but only to himself. (How 'friendly' were they?) It couldn't be true, though, he thought, as he paddled in the comforting water. Simon looked so fit now, so tanned. It was all some sort of dream or nightmare or hoax. He wondered what Andrea had to tell him.

Susie was sitting crooning over Peaches. The kitten was almost a cat now, and had developed the slinky walk of a hunter. But now she was pretending to be a baby again, lying on Susie's lap and sucking her finger. David watched. He could imagine Susie with four children: there was something patient-looking, maternal, about her already.

He'd been trying all day to tell his mother about Andrea coming. So far, it was only Susie he'd told. He'd have to get it over with.

He went out to her study. 'Okay if there's one extra for tea?' He tried to make it sound casual but his voice came out as a kind of squeak.

His mother looked up, surprised. 'Simon? Of course. I expect him to be here.'

David had forgotten about Simon. '*Two* extra for tea.'

She looked at his flushed face. 'You mean that girl.'

He nodded, miserably.

'Of course, if you like.'

'You don't sound too keen.'

'Well, it's not much warning, David. I'd have laid it on a bit if I'd thought you were inviting your girl for tea.'

'She's not my girl.' David felt prickly and anxious whenever he thought of Andrea. He didn't want her prying into his life, into his family. 'Maybe we could go out to tea?'

'Too expensive.'

'I mean, before she comes. Just to the Pizza Hut or something.'

His mother stared at him as if he'd gone mad. 'You can't invite the girl and then run away.'

'I didn't invite her.'

His mother sighed. 'Is that why you've been behaving so oddly lately? These modern girls. I'll never understand them. Still, she must really like you, David, to suggest it.'

The doorbell rang. David rushed to answer it, just in case. He was burning with irritation, as if he'd been trying to thread a needle all day, and missing. Andrea always seemed to put him in a false position. 'Only twice,' a voice said calmingly within him. 'Don't exaggerate.'

But it was Greg who stood there, slouching in a sexual sort of way in the doorway, blocking out the sun. David stared up at him, his irritation gathering into a ball that now had a target. 'Look, if it's Sue you're after, she's busy.'

'Oh?' Greg smiled at him, a lazy, contemptuous smile. 'What's she busy at, then?'

'Nothing to do with you. *She's* nothing to do with you.'

'That's for her to say.' He smiled again, that same, sneering smile. 'Get her, kid.'

David's irritation flared into rage. 'Don't call me "kid". You can just rack off. Leave her alone.'

But Greg had started to make his own way in; started to walk

145

past him as if he weren't even there. David, shaking with anger, pushed him back. He would have liked to lift him in the air, dump him out on the gravel. He struggled to shut the door in his face. But Greg swung it right back, hitting David on the shoulder.

'Get out!' he yelled. 'And don't go bloody hanging around at school waiting for her either.'

'It's all right, Dave.' Gently, Susie nudged him aside. She was still cradling Peaches in her arms.

He came back fuming to the lounge, but, unable to keep still, went out the back door, jumped the fence and ran down the back lane. Soon I won't even be here, he thought. I won't be here to protect her from creeps like Greg. Even when I am here, his other voice told him, she doesn't really need me. His feet pounded up and down on the hard paths until, exhausted, he ran more slowly, in a steady rhythm, round and round the streets he had known since a child.

The whole day had been glorious – another golden autumn day. Warm, almost incredibly so, for this time of the year. But, as the light faded, and a matt orange spread out across the western sky, a crisp coolness set it. Soon it would be quite cold, the overnight temperature as low as eight. A plane with its lights in spasm flew over, far brighter than the brightest stars. David was still waiting, now at the gate, for Andrea.

He would head her off somehow, even tell her she wasn't welcome. Which she wasn't. Yet his stomach twisted into knots at the mere idea of saying it. And, in a way she was, welcome. He would like to see how she seemed in the context of his home. She was the most interesting, unpredictable, *dangerous* person he had ever met. But, at the same time, he wanted to keep her away from Susie and Simon. Protect them from her. She could only be some sort of a spy.

He swung backwards and forwards on the gate as he had done as a child. He'd been here since 5.30, in case she'd be early. His mother and Susie were busy inside, trying to make a nicer tea, he

146

knew, without actually having to go to the shops. They were doing it for him: 'for his girl', as his mum would be putting it to herself. Nobody's girl, Andrea. Or everybody's. No need now only to imagine what she would look like in swimming gear.

6.10. She certainly wasn't going to be early. Silly of him to think so. From the way she walked he'd have thought she'd be a lackadaisical sort of a person. Her hurry that day had not seemed in character. Lackadaisical, careless, detached, that's how he would have pigeonholed her. He thought he was good at characters on the whole, real-life characters.

6.20. No wonder Simon no longer wore a watch. To see the seconds, the minutes, disappear as if they had never been. He wondered how many minutes he had lived, and how many of them he could remember or had left some sort of a trace. 'My life', he thought, imagining it as a straight line of incidents. But when he tried to put them in, most of the line stayed blank.

6.30. Girls. Maybe she wasn't going to come after all. Now he was starting to feel just as annoyed about that as he'd been annoyed about her wanting and going to come. It was cold now. He stopped swinging, rubbed his arms up and down.

6.40. He was getting wild again. Maybe her letter had just been another of her tricks. A cruel trick as he thought of his mother and Susie inside, poring over the dinner, trying to keep it hot without letting it go crisp and dry. He pictured Susie's apple sponge slowly sinking, subsiding into something far more ordinary than she'd intended.

6.45. He was absolutely frozen by now and fed up. Why was he wasting time out here when he could be inside with Susie, just about the opposite of everything Andrea seemed to be? He shut the gate with a vicious bang and ran up the path, locking the wire screen and front door behind him. No one else would be coming in tonight.

'Oh there you are.' His mother came out to meet him, her face hot from the stove. 'No sign of her? Maybe you could give her a ring.'

147

'Don't know her number. Not even her address.' His voice was rigid with tension.

'Oh.' She patted him kindly on the arm. 'Let's wait till seven then, shall we? If she's not here by then, we'll really have to begin.'

Susie and Simon were playing Scrabble, peacefully, in the lounge. David looked down, with irritation, at the two blond heads. How could they be playing Scrabble at a time like this? How could Simon be playing a game with some of his last few precious minutes? They were good at it, though. He bent down to see what large words were holding the board out so well in so many directions. That was a good one, he thought, looking at a ten-letter word spread helpfully across the centre of the board with smaller words branching off from it. 'Experiment'.

'I thought eight letters were the most you could have,' he said. 'Or is it less?'

Right on seven, the phone rang. David rushed for it, then stood for a second getting his breathing back into some sort of order. 'Hello,' he said, equably, calmly. But the call was for his mother.

He checked his watch. 7.05. He felt his anger rise again; and at that moment, the doorbell rang.

But his anger evaporated when he saw her. He had never seen her look ... vulnerable, before. She must have been in a fight. She had a bruise just under her eye, and when she moved towards him, he could see she was limping. The elegant walk, gone. She was wearing a green patterned shirt and an olive jacket over it, but the top buttons of the shirt were in the wrong holes. He tried not to think of why.

'Hi, Yes, I know,' she said, as he continued to stare at her. 'A mess. I got held up – or down, you might say. But I had to come.'

'Had to'. What did she mean? She was carrying a folder under her arm. It looked dirty, torn, as if it had been in a fight too.

He led her down the passage and into the lounge. But everyone had gone into the kitchen. His mother had started to serve up the meal. She put the serving dish down as soon as she saw Andrea, and gave her both her hands. Only a flicker of her eyelid

148

showed David she had actually noticed that Andrea looked a wreck. Simon was standing up and Susie was staring at her unabashed. 'My friend Andrea,' he said, putting his hand under her elbow and leading her gently to the seat next to his mother and opposite where he would sit. She placed the folder on the sideboard beside her.

'We'd just given up on you.' His mother served her a huge plate of lasagne and set the salad bowl in front of her. 'I'm so glad you could come.'

David could see that Simon was trying to think of something polite to say but had run out of ideas. He too was staring at the displaced buttons. 'I'm Simon,' he said at last. 'Hope you like Italian food. We're so pleased we've learnt how to do it, we make it all the time.'

'Mum all the time. You sometimes. I've made the pudding,' Susie announced confidentially to Andrea. 'You have to eat some of that.'

Andrea smiled at her, the warmest, most natural smile David had ever seen her give. 'I certainly will. I'll enjoy eating with a family. I'm the only one at home.'

'You live alone?'

Andrea turned to David's mother, who had stopped serving out and was now herself sitting down to eat . 'The only child, I meant. I live with my father.'

'At Largs,' Simon said, and then blushed, thinking he'd said the wrong thing.

This time it was Andrea who blushed. David wished he hadn't told Simon anything. She'd think he'd told him everything – which he hadn't. Not exactly. He talked furiously to cover it up. 'It's really nice down there. I'd forgotten how good the beach is. Wide, and with some tussock grass still, like it must all have been once. Even a few sandhills.'

'I've always liked it,' said Andrea, 'but the place has got a bit rough the last year or two. We've been broken into twice, and the shop on the corner just about every week in the summer holidays.'

149

'Do you have a mother?' David longed to ask. 'What does your father do?' 'Do you work?' '*Where* do you work?' 'Who do you work for?' 'Why do you spend all this time following me around?' 'Who gave you that black eye?'

Luckily he had Susie. 'I'm still at school,' she said. 'What about you?'

'No. I left last year.' And then, as Susie kept looking at her, waiting for more, 'I've got a sort of secretarial job, I suppose you could describe it as. Nothing too heavy.' (At The House of Records? Or, 'outsourcing' for them?) 'I might go to uni later, but I got sick of studying.'

'More salad, Andrea?' asked his mum. 'I can see there's no point in offering you more lasagne.'

Andrea had eaten about half of hers, but had not attempted to disguise the fact. The half sat uneaten, centrally on her plate. 'I couldn't really. I need to save a small place for dessert.'

Susie went over to inspect it. 'It might be a tiny bit overdone.' It was the kind of apple sponge you could do on top of the stove. You cooked the apple then poured the cake mixture over it. You weren't supposed to look at it till it was finished, so that it was always a bit frightening, wondering if it had turned out. 'It's sinking a bit in the middle, but I'll give you a nice crisp piece at the edge. You can have more if you want. Cream or icecream?'

'Could I be greedy and say both?'

David's mother beamed. She liked people to be greedy.

Susie chatted on about school and hockey and about her kitten Peaches, and how Dave wouldn't let her have Cream, the matching kitten, so it wasn't really obvious that David and Simon and Andrea were rather quiet. Andrea did try to draw them out a bit, though, latterly.

'And you, Simon, what winter sports do you play or are you the armchair type? Not that you look it.'

'I used to play football.'

She waited, but he didn't add anything.

'And David. You'll just be concentrating on Year 12?'

150

If only that were all he had to worry him.

At times, Andrea shifted uneasily in her seat. She might be in pain, David thought.

After coffee and a chocolate which his mother had dug out from somewhere, Andrea whispered to him: 'There's something I have to show you.' She picked up the folder, lying on the sideboard. 'Some place else.'

He led the way up the stairs to his room.

'Lovely,' she said, looking around. 'I like pine especially.' She put the folder down on his desk. 'The article inside is classified. But I've taken a copy. Without permission, of course. Once you've read it, destroy it. Don't show it to anyone first. Don't mention it either.' She paused. 'Not even to Simon. *Promise.*'

She sounded as urgent as anyone could who looked so tired, so sore. He stared at her. She meant it. She was serious. What sort of trouble could she get into? He suspected roughing up would be nothing to it. 'Okay.' Solemnly he put the folder in the second to bottom drawer of his desk.

'And now,' she said quickly, before he could ask her questions about it, 'I'll really have to go.' She looked terrible: worn, defeated. He could see it had even been an effort for her getting up the attic stairs.

David farewelled her at the gate.

'Thanks,' she said. 'Especially thanks for not asking about the black eye. You've been lucky, having a family like that.'

It was only later that he wondered about her choice of tense.

chapter 31

DAVID BELTED UP the stairs, opened the drawer, and turned the folder over slowly in his hands. Was this the key? He took out the article, smoothed it down. It too was torn, dirty, battered-looking, like the folder. Like Andrea. Had the fight somehow been about this?

Heart racing, he skimmed the pages. It was about due dates, all right. Some parts leapt out at him. *It has only been the ostrich-like nature of the general public – not wanting to know – that has prevented this* (the release of information about probable due dates) *from becoming a contentious issue.*

He read further. It was about the *effect* on people who had been told *or who had been allowed to find out* about their projected due date.

It is remarkable how often, in those cases, the proposed 'due date' (which can only be an approximation at best), has yielded a positive result: i.e. the proposed due date and the actual expiry date have been identical. It has been suggested (Holl and Stott, 1997), that this must be, at least in part, an effect of the experiment itself: of people being aware of their supposed due date. Perhaps in these cases we could, in fact (and ruling out the possibility of anything more sinister), see the fulfilment of this date as a kind of induced suicide.

How he would love to show the article to Simon, or at least discuss it with him! But there, he had promised. And there was surely no more likelihood in Simon's case than in his own, of their being induced by their due date, or anything else, to commit suicide. He read it through once more, then tore it up into infinitely small pieces.

He was relieved when Andrea rang during the week, suggesting they see a film at the Windsor. But when Friday night came, she wouldn't talk to him about the article.

'I'll just say one thing,' she said, 'and it must be obvious already. Fate, you know, I'm not sure about. It might be worth fighting back at it. In any case, what would there be to lose?'

And that was it. After that, trivia.

He felt very aware of her, in the cinema. His arm actually trembled, where it met hers, but she showed no sign of being similarly affected. She'd gone back to being quite distant. Cool. Reserved.

There seemed to be no chance of her repeating the earlier performance, in her house. He was the one who kept thinking about it, obsessively: about her undoing the buttons of the soft blouse. About the buttons of the patterned green shirt being in the wrong holes on Sunday night at dinner. Who had done that? But he couldn't ask – not after she'd thanked him for *not* asking. Being with her, he felt uneasy, as he always did. But it was an uneasiness edged with excitement. And she was trying to help him. Wasn't she?

After the film, they walked down to the sea-wall. He longed to touch her. It was the way she walked, with so much assurance, that held him back. Even to have run his hand up the inside of her arm, even that would have eased him.

He tried to pull his mind back to what was important. The days were running out, faster and faster. Nine days. He cleared his throat. 'What does your father do?' She didn't answer. Just tossed her head and walked on. 'Does he have an interesting job?'

'You could say so. Quite interesting. He's a kind of clerk, I suppose.'

Why did she only 'suppose'? 'Does he work at The . . .'

'Ask me no questions . . .'

Was that telling him he did, or he didn't?

She changed the subject then. Or had she? 'How's your friend? The retired footballer. Does he seem okay?'

'Why shouldn't he be?' And then, suspicious again, 'What do you know about Simon?'

'Only what you've told me.'

They walked out, over the sea. It was rough, cold. The waves were breaking far out from shore, slapping in at the end of the jetty, sending up a fine spray that went all over them. There was no one else around. It had started to rain as well. Yet she wouldn't run for shelter, or even go into the shelter nearby. She stood, out at the end of the jetty, hanging onto the rail.

There was something so unpredictable about her. Her mood seemed to change with the mood of the sea: she became less contained, *wilder*. It suited him. Her hair (always auburn now)

153

fell in rat's-tails on her shoulders, her shirt clung into her. He sensed the difference, and put his arm around her, pulling her to him. Bending down, he tasted salt on her cheek. And she'd clung to him: there was no other word for it. Clung to him at the end of the jetty with the salt water spraying up and the rain water cascading down. Above them, seagulls blew around, their calls harsh and hollow. He pushed her hair back from her face – and he could have sworn, amidst all the other water, there were tears in her eyes.

'Does it always creak like that?'

'What?' he asked, his head buried in her hair.

'The jetty. Does it always creak like that?'

He listened. Under the sound of the waves and wind he could hear it: the creaking of old wood, old timbers. 'Don't know. It's not often rough like this.'

At the end of the long drive back he tried to talk to her about what she'd said earlier. 'Andrea, what did you mean about Fate? How could you fight it back?'

She got out of the car then, key poised, ready to let herself in. He followed her up to the gate. The house lay in darkness.

He put his hand over hers, over the latch of the gate. His voice came out urgent, hoarse. 'You've got to tell me what you mean.'

She laughed then, a light, high laugh. He could feel the distance between them again. 'I don't have to, anything.' And ran up the path. As she did so, a light came on inside.

chapter 32

THE NEXT DAY David was going away for the weekend with Simon. Just the two of them. Their last 'safe' weekend. 'This friend of Mum's will lend us their shack at Middleton. Then we won't have to appear normal.'

154

They'd decided not to tell their families, not even now. If they told them, they would lose their freedom: lose all pretence of an ordinary life. It was more than that too. They both felt superstitious about it: if they told other people, it would make it real. It would *sound* theatrical, but it would make it happen.

David laughed at what Simon had said, even though it was true. The problem of appearing normal was increasing as the date drew near. David knew his mother was amazed at his unexpected outbursts of rage, when he couldn't have the car when he wanted it, for example, or when she'd got the letter from school about his absenteeism.

'I'm really disappointed in you, David,' she'd said. 'Your last year. You know how important it is. And you're so good at your work. It's such a waste. The cards are stacked against all you young people as it is, without making it worse.'

He knew he sounded ridiculous, even as he stormed around. 'Leave me alone! I don't have to go to school. It's my life!' All the clichés. He was horrified to find that when he got upset about anything, all he could do was spout the most awful clichés.

Then there was the play Susie had been in at school. It was only a small part, but still it *was* a part and he knew his mum sensed his reluctance. 'It's only common politeness.'

He decided he would go, in spite of what his mother said. 'Mum, I'm going. But not because of what you've said. I just wish you'd leave me alone.'

His mother looked genuinely upset. 'Really, David. I don't know how to talk to you any more. I thought we'd missed out on all this dreadful teenage business.'

It would be a relief to get away with Simon.

It was another unbelievable day when they left: still warm, still golden. His mother and Susie came out to see them off. 'Lucky things,' said Susie, half angling for an invitation. But it wasn't going to come. Simon bent over the car boot, rearranging their gear inside it, then slammed it shut. They stepped into the car with a feeling of ceremony and adventure greater than the occasion seemed to warrant. David was glad his mum and Susie were still waiting at the gate as Simon turned the car further up the street and drove back. He felt his heart tug at him, then fill with a helpless yearning as Susie and his mum got smaller, and the house and the park disappeared. A kind of preview of what it was going to be like.

'I'm worried about my mother,' said Simon, as they headed south out of the denser suburbs. 'She's been so happy lately with me seeming better. It's very hard.'

David thought about what Simon had said. It made him feel guilty, mainly. 'I haven't thought much about anybody else, except you. You're taking it much better than me.'

'Only because I've got less to lose.' His laugh was bitter. 'It's far worse for you. These huge doses of radiotherapy they give us, you don't know what you'd be like in later life. Damaged, for sure. At least I escaped the chemo. Sometimes you wonder if you can be bothered living on in a body that's wrecked. I think about that often. Lisa's brother knew he'd be infertile. Anyway, I've had longer to get used to the idea. That's all.'

'And you accept it. I still keep thinking it can't be true. That even if it is, there must be some way of avoiding it.'

'That's what I thought we should work out this weekend. A strategy for dealing with the day. We could go on one of those mystery flights or something – I've always wanted to do that. Or would that endanger other people? Maybe you can't avoid your fate, but at least you can have a try at it. Some brown leaves gave me the idea.' He laughed.

'Leaves?'

'There were these huge crisp leaves in Dequetteville Terrace – when I was going for my treatment. They kept daring the cars. Bowling along in front of them; playing games, as if they were stronger.'

But David was thinking about Andrea. What Simon had said about Fate, it was the same sort of thing she'd said. He put the window fully down and let the mild wind blow through him. He

156

dabbled his hands in the drafts of air and looked at the dry paddocks that stretched out on either side of them. He felt completely relaxed when Simon was driving. They were approaching the wind tunnel which he'd crossed at a reckless speed that day he'd been followed by Andrea. But Simon slowed down, was caring for their lives as if they had a future.

David said cautiously, 'Maybe *believing* you know your fate is a bit like someone pointing the bone? It's the knowing it, brings it on?'

'And not Fate itself? Maybe. You're getting too subtle for me.'

The Middleton 'shack' was far grander than he'd imagined. It angled itself towards the sea, but was several streets back. Vacant blocks still lay in front of it. Freshly painted weatherboard with cream walls and dark brown woodwork. It looked welcoming, its garden neat, even manicured. Magpies warbled idyllically in the she-oaks by the gate. David walked in, feeling at home at once.

The door opened into the lounge with comfortable old-style couches and chairs, coffee tables with magazines and a shelf of books. Two bedrooms were on the left, up a passage, with the bathroom and laundry opposite. A third bedroom lay up at the end and faced out onto the back garden. David dumped his bag in the first bedroom where Simon had already left his, and walked through to the kitchen-dining room area. 'Mind if we share a room?' He didn't feel like being alone. 'This is great.' He knew already it had the peaceful feel of his favourite places.

Simon was bustling around, looking in cupboards, putting the jug on for coffee. They'd bought rolls and biscuits and cakes at the bakery at Mount Compass on the way through, and sausages and bacon at the butcher's. Nothing too fancy, nothing too hard. They had planned to do absolutely nothing but read and soak up the sun.

David looked warmly at him. Simon had always been the busy one, the doer, the organiser, the one with the ideas. The funny one. Perhaps that was what he should have picked up on first: Simon had ceased to be funny. Maybe he'd had it radiated out of him.

Simon looked glumly up at the large, definite-looking kitchen clock with its dark brown edging. 'Even here, *time, like an everlasting stream* . . . More like a hammer, really. You wouldn't think you'd need a second hand in the country.'

'Just standard.'

'There should be different kinds of clocks: clocks that measure different things.'

'Like what?'

'Well, what you get out of it rather than just this steady tick-tock-ing as if each "tick" is the same as the next "tock". Different time rates for different things. Speeded up for dentist days, and so on.'

'But time never does seem steady. Bits always used to drag.'

David was becoming familiar with the waves of panic that would suddenly sweep over him. They were more frequent now, now that the days grew less. Eight. What could you do with eight days? Only the length of a holiday. He'd been feeling perfectly all right, sipping his coffee with Simon, solid, reassuring opposite, and then suddenly he'd had a rush of fear, and the sense that he would simply have to get outside. How Simon had felt at Cleland that time – belting off amidst the kangaroos.

On one side, Middleton was a surfing beach; black-clad surfers were riding it out on what waves there were. But with Simon following, David headed the other way, to the walking beach with its small rocks and seaweed and brownish sand. He stopped, let some of it trickle through his fingers.

Simon strode on, a little in front, picking up a stone now and then and skimming it across the waves. He was wearing white shorts and a light yellow top, almost the colour of his hair. He looked like an ad for health or longevity or whatever. David picked up a stone and sent it viciously into the waves. His green shirt and silver shorts showed darker splashes.

He caught up with Simon. 'Suppose this was a novel. You have to work out the ending.'

'Your mother's son. I've gone off fiction.'

'No, seriously. It might give us an idea of how to behave if we thought of it as a story.'

'A way to behave or a way to escape?'

'Escape is what I hope, I guess.'

Simon sat down on a rock. David stood beside him, positioning himself so that the sun shone at his back – and wondering why he bothered. 'It's what we have to work out. You said (in the car coming down) we'd have to work it out.'

Simon looked up at him. 'Should we be together or separate? That's the first question. Should we stay in one house or two? Or not at home at all in case that brings trucks into the lounge or lightning strikes or whatever else.'

'That sounds fantastic – and so unlikely. Home always seems safest. I'd hate to be alone.'

'Perhaps that's just playing into the hands of fate. To be together. It has to work twice as hard if we're separate.'

'I guess you're right. Then again, maybe there's no point in having any sort of a plan.'

For the spell of the sea was starting to work. David could feel all urgency leave his mind, as he could tell it was leaving Simon's, from the increasingly fixed way in which he looked out at the waves. David listened to the constant lapping of the water on the rocks, to the cry of the gulls, to the wash of the waves on pebbles. He smelt the seaweed; everywhere the fresh briny smell of the sea. He watched the waves, far – far, far out, breaking with white tips, and took no notice at all of the man in sunglasses, picking up shells by the shore.

chapter 33

THEY'D FINISHED AN early tea and were watching the magpies finishing theirs. David's face felt cracked and dry from the sun.

'There's that character again,' said Simon. 'The one who was watching us on the beach.'

A tall, dark-haired man in sunglasses was walking past on the other side of the street.

'Who's paranoid now?' said David, yet shuddering, believing it at the same time. He'd seen that man before, at another beach. Tracked down, even here, like animals at bay.

The stranger walked on.

Simon moved away from the window. 'I've been wanting to ask you something. Would you really rather not have known? I feel responsible. If it hadn't been for me and my stupid dare . . .'

David's mind filled with images. Of Susie in her pink fluorescent two-piece, laughing by the pool; of his mother, pulling out her endless manuscripts; of the sky in the early morning; of hanging over the gate at sunset, waiting for Andrea; of Simon striding along the beach, with his matching shirt and hair. He wouldn't really have noticed any of that. He wouldn't even have *met* Andrea. His heart flooded with the thought of her, clinging to him on the jetty that creaked in the wind. And he'd tried to see his dad. Some things you couldn't arrange, some things you just couldn't finish off. He sighed. 'No. I'm glad. I think I'm glad. Terrified, too.'

Simon turned on the TV, but it was black and white, and not terribly clear. He switched it off again. 'It was only avoidance behaviour anyway. I think I'll write some letters instead.'

'Who's away?'

'Nobody. To Mum, and that. For after.'

David felt a shiver go up his back. Another cliché reaction, but it was his and he could feel it. Death was something that happened to other people: never to oneself.

'Maybe you should, too. Write to Susie at least. It's going to be awful for her. And for your mother, of course.'

But the idea had an unreality about it that David couldn't come to terms with. Last letters, when he was perfectly fit and well; when, after all, it might be some sort of hoax or mistake.

160

Then a thought came to him. 'You start leaving all these notes around, people'll say it was suicide.'

Simon looked uncomprehending.

'If the car crashes, say. They'll think you aimed up a tree.'

'Mm. Yeah.' Simon chewed on his pen. 'No one'll think that, not the way I'll put it. And I'll back date it to when I first knew I was ill.'

Simon sat intent, his blond head down, scribbling away. David remembered how Simon had loved acting, when they were younger. They were always playing at pirates, or sailors lost at sea, and later, spacemen who'd lost touch with earth. Perhaps that's what they were playing now? Maybe this was just another role for him; another part to play. Perhaps the reality of it hadn't touched him.

'You know when we played *Nightmare* last time, and you put "long corridors" as your greatest fear . . .'

Simon looked up.

'At the time I thought you meant The House of Records. But it was the hospital, wasn't it?'

Simon nodded.

'Why "your greatest fear"?'

'It's not the corridor, I suppose, it's just what it comes to suggest. You go down there, for the radiotherapy, every day – every weekday. Cancer goes to sleep at weekends.'

'And . . .'

'Well, you wait, wait around in long queues to go on the machine. Look at all the other people standing about, most of them much older than you. They stare at you, or seem to, because you're so much younger, I guess. Then it's your turn.'

Simon seemed to have stopped. He even picked up his pen again.

'Go on.'

'You put on a gown – bluish, unless they've run out, rusty pink for the women, and they put you on a bed: narrow, really narrow, and arrange you on it in complicated positions. Put your arms in slings and pads, strap you down so you won't move. Then they say, "Don't move at all," and run from the room. Leave you to it. And the machine, humming in a pleased way, comes down over you.

161

Sometimes it's so long, you think they've forgotten about you, and you'll be burnt right through. There's a clock, of course. You lie still and watch the clock. The room's completely white: the walls, the bed, even the clock. And music plays – musak, sickly sweet.'

'It sounds awful. Like a torture chamber. Futuristic.'

'All your cells in the area under the machine are being destroyed. The healthy ones as well. One time I thought I'd have to run from the bed, it seemed so long.'

David sighed. And there he was, thinking Simon hadn't faced up to the reality of what was to happen. He'd already had far more reality than David would ever see. He wished he'd noticed at the time. Why hadn't he noticed more?

'And then there're the old people. Can you imagine it? Your mother, my mother in thirty years' time. People that old having to go through it. Brought in, in ambulances, from nursing homes. Wheeled in, wheeled out. That's the only thing I can think of: it's easier to take, being younger. No one old should have to go through that. And then, of course, when you're back at school. Nobody looks you in the eye any more. You make everyone feel afraid for themselves. It's uncomfortable: they look away. I didn't want that to happen with you. Not that it would've. I just felt . . .'

Simon's head was bent again over his letter. David wished he could tell him what a great friend he'd been. Maybe he could, should, whatever.

'Sime.'

'Mm?'

But he couldn't. He couldn't say it. And perhaps words would diminish it. Simon looked up, pen in hand.

'Nothing. Everything.'

Simon smiled at him. He knew, without his having to say any of it.

That night David dreamt he was running down the beach in the half dark, towards a line of trenches. It was his job to take out the dead soldiers before the rush of live ones hit the shore. He would have to be quick: already he could see fresh boats bobbing about in the grey water. He looked around, but there was no one to help him.

He said to the sergeant, 'I can't carry them out on my own. They'll be heavy.'

As lead. Stiff, like toy soldiers.

The sergeant stared at him, stared out of cold blue eyes. 'No they won't, actually.' He handed him a sandbag. 'You'll find only bits.'

He stood for a moment, feeling himself shake, then turned and tried to run up the beach, up towards the high cliffs, waiting for a blue-eyed bullet to lodge in his back.

'What's the matter?' It was Simon, bending over him, holding onto his arm, *hard*. The bed seemed narrow and he felt as if he were floating up off it. 'You were screaming, well, shouting, any-way. No, *screaming*, I'm sure you were.'

'Sorry. It was this dream . . .'

'Some dream. Can you remember it?'

David creased up his forehead. 'Only bits. Yes, of course. "Bits" is the word.' And he told Simon what he remembered.

'No wonder you were screaming. But they had to do it, didn't they, all those kids?'

'What d'you mean?'

'The ones that were left. That would've been their job: to clear the trenches. Of bits of their friends.'

David shuddered. *His* nightmare had been someone else's real-ity. What if *his* reality . . . ? 'What do you dream about?' he asked quickly.

'Usually, nothing. But when I do . . .'

'Yes?'

'I dream about the other important thing . . .'

(Sex, he must mean. Why not say it?)

' . . . and sometimes about football. It's always the same dream.' He looked away. 'I walk out of this long corridor into the sun. My eyes are dazzled at first. Everything looks misty, but then I see it's a football field. Suddenly I'm free. I'm running with the ball . . .

There aren't any goalposts, so I can keep running, weaving in and out of the shadows of the other players. But then the wind gets up. Rain blows across the ground, and the shadows turn into dry leaves.' He looked at David. 'That's when I know I have to go inside again.'

They drove home the next evening as the sun was setting. Seven days. The trees were turning black against the lower lemon of the sky, and, higher up, faint threads of pink pushed up against the blue. The peaceful time of the day. They had come here to sort out a plan, but almost, in the quiet of the place, they had felt they didn't need one.

Again it was Simon who drove, his hands anchored steadily on the wheel, not flying off it, like Andrea's slender ones. His remarks he addressed carefully to the road in front, not straight to David, as Andrea's often were.

'Seen any more of the girl?' asked Simon, tuning in, as he often seemed to, to David's thoughts.

'We went to the pictures Friday night. Windsor. Interesting.'

'I wasn't wondering about the film especially.'

'No. I like being with her, but I feel uneasy too. Maybe a bit less uneasy than I did. And then I feel it's a waste of time. When I'm with her, I catch myself thinking I should be with Susie, or you.' Yet his heart turned over at the thought of her.

'But she might know something. She *must* know something. And it was funny about all those bruises on her. I don't suppose you could ask her about that?'

David shook his head. And what *did* Andrea know? All the talk, or rather, the little bit of talk, about Fate. Andrea *must* know about his due date. Did she know about Simon's too?

'You're a bit fascinated, if you ask me.'

Of course David hadn't, but it was true: he *was* fascinated by Andrea. In some moods, he wanted to be with her all the time. He clenched his fists. He wanted to *touch* her all the time.

chapter 34

A BLANKNESS FELL over the last days; a kind of numbness over David. He just went through routines. Although the days were so few now, he had started going to school again. He didn't know what else to do. Six days, five days, four . . . His mother saw it as him 'getting back to his old self', but inside, he was totally inert. Sitting at the table with Susie and his mum, he felt as if he were in a glass case. The only times he came partially to life were when Simon was there or Andrea rang. She did this every day when he got home.

'It's Andrea again,' Susie would say, smiling at him sideways.

'Want to take a lonely girl to the beach? Into town? Skating?' Andrea would say. In a way, strangely, he preferred talking to her over the phone. She sounded so close to him then, her voice intimate, musical. He loved its modulations. There was something too about the way she talked that he liked – not just her voice, but her . . . syntax, he supposed Western would call it. She held things back. She would keep the main thought in her sentence to the end as if she were speaking in German, perhaps. 'All day I'll be busy,' she'd say. 'But at *Café Paradiso*, I'll meet you. After work.'

'*Paradiso*'. A name he could do without.

She'd been taking his arm, when they went out. Sometimes his hand. He could see people looking at them, especially at Andrea. Always so poised, so beautifully groomed in greens and yellows, burnt orange and lime, her head bent forward, ever so slightly, the way she always walked.

His mother was anxious. 'Your most important year at school,' she would say as he'd go out again. 'Slow it down; steady on. There'll be plenty of time at the end of the year.'

('Plenty of time'? 'The end of the year'?)

They took his bike on Wednesday, when his mum had the car.

Andrea rode on the carrier. His shirt blew out in the wind. She grabbed the shirt in her hands and buried her head in the small of his back. He wobbled a bit, nearly fell off.

It was Simon who was doing the planning. At first he'd thought they should go camping for the weekend on which it was (*next weekend!*), but the weather looked as if it'd broken and it would seem odd weather for that. It would raise questions. And now the due date seemed even more a kind of crime. Something to be kept hidden. Yet they wanted to go off somewhere so that, whatever it was, couldn't happen to anyone else. They couldn't, they decided, just skulk at home.

But, at the end, it turned out not to have been a problem at all, just like clouds dispersing before his last athletics' carnival. Everyone would be away that Sunday: Simon's mother on a business trip with his dad, David's mother bushwalking. Even Susie would be away. She was staying down at Christies Beach in a caravan park with Cynth and her parents; Cynthia now a lot better, and in need of sea air. Almost like fate.

The two boys would have both houses to themselves, or, if they liked, one house each. They decided, finally, on one house each. That would spread the risk.

Thursday.

Three days.

Simon coughed nervously. 'I've got a funny feeling about the day, as if it's not going to be what we've imagined.'

'Nothing ever is. But what have we imagined?'

David had put up a block himself, so that now he was living from day to day, from minute to minute. He wasn't imagining anything, although his sleep was becoming more and more disturbed. Elongated hopelessness, was what he thought each morning. Grey water. The feeling of Simon's own endless corridors.

Simon was answering him. 'I'm not sure. Something cosmic. A meteor. A lightning strike. Something dramatic.'

David sighed. He felt too ordinary for dramatic death. Too young for death of any kind. 'I'm going to lie on my bed all day.

Reading. Whatever it is will have to come and get me.' But even as he said it, he knew the phrase suggested he was thinking of it still as some sort of game, some sort of *Nightmare*.

His happiest outing, in that last week, was not with Simon, or Andrea, but with his mum and Susie to the market on Friday night. Friday, June the 12th. Two days. That was all that was left.

Yet still the market made David feel safe: stall after stall of fresh vegetables and fruit, the owners yelling out their special bargain prices. Normal things. Little things. Stalls of cheeses and continental meats, cut flowers and bulbs, bread of all shapes and sizes, soft and crusty rolls. They passed the stall up the far end with its sheepskin rugs made out of oddments, formed into squares, that they'd bought for Ged when he'd been a pup. Then the meat shops, the coffee shop with its bustle, its chatter and inviting, warming smell. Everywhere was purpose and busyness. He watched the escalator, a bit like time itself, moving up to the car park with the people going home. But, for a while, he felt part of everything. He stuffed the juiciest pears, the reddest apples into his mum's hessian bag as if it really mattered.

Now Susie was down at the paper end of the market, going through a pile of the cheap writing pads they kept. She always liked to have plenty of scrap paper for drawing on and 'just for thinking with'. She loved the market. They kept losing her among the stalls, but when she'd disappeared for an especially long time, his mum headed for the pet shop. David's heart contracted when he saw her. Sure enough, there she was, poking her fingers through the wire at a straggly pup. She looked up in a pleading way. 'One day,' said her mum, 'when we've a proper fence up.'

'But he's such a baby. And no one'll want him. He looks as if he's been here for ages.'

The puppy looked out with bleary eyes that seemed to hold a faint sparkle of hope returning. Through the bars he was sucking on one of Susie's fingers. Then he wagged his tail and barked frailly, unusedly. 'Look at me,' he seemed to be saying. 'I'm a good dog, a useful dog. Marketable.'

David drew his mum away, out of the shop. It would be something for Susie. 'Let her have it, Mum,' he whispered. 'I'll pay with the rest of my car money.'

She shook her head.

'And the injections, desexing and so on. Honest.' He'd been carrying a ridiculous amount of money around all week.

They watched Susie through the glass. She knelt motionless, absorbed.

'But she'll always be wanting to rescue something. And then, she'll be away this weekend.'

He could see his mum was weakening, her reasons or excuses getting smaller.

'And I wanted to take you both to *Paul's*.'

There it was: the flimsiest excuse of all. 'Great. I'll tell her, shall I? And we can still go to *Paul's*. I'll get the man to hold him till we get back. No, Mum, we don't need a basket for him. A carton will be fine. He doesn't look as if he'd have the strength to get out of it.'

He strode back into the shop. 'We'll have him. How much?' He knew he should have said it the other way round, but it was too late now. A musty smell of straw filled the air.

Susie scrambled up. The puppy looked bereft, still with its tongue half out, ready to lick. 'What're you doing?'

David flashed his bank notes. 'What's it look like?'

'But Mum, what's she going to say?'

'She's already said. It's okay. He's yours.' He turned to the man. 'We'll be back for him inside an hour.'

The shopkeeper nodded, looking pleased in excess of the situation, David thought. It *had* been there a long time. Probably flea-ridden. Still, it was a pleasant sort of a mutt: earnest eyes and a funny way of holding its head. Like Andrea. He suppressed a laugh. It held its neck out forward, in the very same way.

It was hard, getting Susie to leave the puppy. In the end his mum reassured her, cruelly. 'No one else is going to want it.'

168

He'd said, 'Anyway, he's paid for.' And he shunted her out of the shop.

Then they'd gone to *Paul's*, for the best fish and chips in Adelaide. It had given him that secure feeling again, sitting there where they'd sat so often when he and Sue had been much younger. He remembered as a child the huge plates of bread, already buttered, that came before your meal. Now he and Susie ate the bread up quickly so that the waitress would get them more, just as had happened when they'd been small. His mum was even having a small glass of wine, 'to celebrate the new addition. You can drive back, David.'

'What're you going to call him?'

Susie ate her fourth piece of bread and butter with practised ease. She always smiled a lot, but now she couldn't stop. She smiled into the bread and butter, into the vinegar bottle, and widely, at anyone who approached. People would be thinking she was the one with the wine and not the mineral water she steadily ordered when she was out. 'Goffie,' she said at last.

'"Goffie"! What sort of name is that?'

'I don't know. It sort of came to me. I like it. I like the sound of it.'

That would be it, then. 'Goffie'. Susie was always perfectly definite: you could always count on Susie knowing her own mind. And never changing it. Except about possible careers.

Huge plates of garfish in batter and big white straight chips were put in front of them. Salad teetered around at the edge. *Paul's* was quite dark, the walls black with a strip of deep red high up. It was busy and rowdy and homey. The cooks, in black-and-white striped aprons, were in full view, perspiring over the hot-plates and pans. The window in front of them was full of the choicest, whitest, thickest garfish and whiting fillets. The door clanged constantly as the restaurant filled up. He and Susie ate as quickly as they could, before the succulent chips grew cold. Their mother came along more slowly, delicately, behind. He sat back, drank the rest of his orange squash and ordered another. I'm happy, he thought, amazed at himself. I'm part of it all once more. But even as he thought it he was aware of his mind, at it again, taking a snapshot of the scene.

chapter 35

IT WAS SATURDAY night. Perhaps their *last* night. Saturday, the 13th of June. The night before their due date. David and Simon had gone to *Grimaldi's* for tea, then out to Magill to see a film, just as if it were any other Saturday night. Now they were back at Simon's for supper.

His mother was happy to see them back. She fussed around, got them hot chocolate with marshmallows melting in it, as though they'd been small boys again. She'd been baking too: almond biscuits and banana cake. David, feeling sick, could sense his stomach ballooning out as he ate. 'And tell me about the film,' she was saying. 'What was it like?' Everything was back to normal for her. And she was so proud of Simon, looking up at him as he'd come in, blond, tall, through the doorway, even having to bend down, or imagining that he had to, to get through it. David almost choked a couple of times on his biscuits, yet he'd eaten steadily on, knowing it was only a little, but something he could do that would give her pleasure.

'I don't know. What did *you* think of the film?' Simon asked him. 'It seemed a bit mild, a bit washed-out to me.'

'Maybe we just weren't in the mood.'

Simon's mum looked puzzled, as they both laughed as at some extravagant joke. But then joined in, laughed too.

Simon came with him to the gate. 'The main thing is, don't leave the house on any account. And I won't leave mine.'

They both must have been on some sort of high. It was only after he'd driven off that David realised he might never see Simon again.

He woke up normally at 7am. Not 'as usual', that wasn't what he meant. 'Normally'. Feeling normal. Like it was any other day. The sun was already streaming into the attic, although it came and went, so there was plenty of cloud around. He could hear the puppy starting to give baby yaps from Susie's room. She'd insisted it sleep in there till she got back so that it would know she was coming. It seemed strange reasoning to him.

He put his feet down on the pine floor and the room spun around, as if it were one of those revolving restaurants set on high speed. I just sat up too suddenly, he thought. But when he repeated the process, it happened again. The yapping was becoming frantic. He staggered downstairs and the pup ran towards him, wriggling, writhing almost, against his legs. He picked it up, and it squirmed against him happily, raising its tiny blond head, licking his chin with a soft little tongue. Still holding it, he got out its bowl and one of the meals Susie had carefully packaged. 'Goffie – breakfast', he read on the label. She'd even colour-coded each one. Yellow ribbon meant breakfast, green ribbon meant lunch, and the larger, red-coded bag was for tea. There was even a tiny mauve-ribboned package labelled 'Supper, if required'.

Goffie bolted his breakfast, nearly eating the yellow ribbon as well. David made a cup of tea, then. Took one in to his mum. But she wasn't there. The bed already made. He felt hollow, exposed, as if his last defence had gone. He checked around the side for the car. But it was still there, its bonnet up, his mum staring thoughtfully in at the engine.

'I can't get it to start. I was just coming to get you.'

But there was little point in asking him. He stared in, just as thoughtfully. Everything seemed in place. 'Better get the RAA. Want me to ring?'

'No time,' said his mother. 'I'll ring Lorna – get her to pick me up instead.'

His mum waited at the gate for her lift. David rushed out with a fresh cup of tea. He thought it was a bit on the milky side, but there. Dropped a kiss on her head. Hugged her hard.

'What's that for? Thanks, dear. But I'll have just a sip.'

David, his throat tight, watched his mum being driven away, waved on and on to her from the gate. Then turned, in a puzzled way, to the car. It had gone perfectly well last night. It was almost as if someone had been tampering with it. Or was he getting para-noid again? He wouldn't ring for road service – filling the day up with complications.

He roamed round the house, not hungry yet, wondering what to do. He felt strangely safe, as if the danger were already over. They'd be laughing at themselves tomorrow for having taken it all so seriously. Like people who believed in forecasts about the end of the world.

It was funny having the house to yourself. It had settled into silence when his mother left. Out of habit he picked up one of the manuscripts lying on her desk and lay on the couch with it. The puppy settled down on his knee. He was actually dozing off.

He woke with a start, feeling cloudy – much less bright than he'd been earlier. He had a shower to revive him, got dressed in his jeans and white T-shirt, and made a big pot of coffee. Then he put on some toast for the smell of it. He looked at his watch. Was that all it was? He wished he could go for a jog. Surely that would be safe enough? Just round the block, jogging carefully on the footpath. Pick up a paper at the deli. But there, he'd promised Simon.

He went out into the dry garden, leaves crackling beneath his feet, and pulled up a few weeds. He wasn't sure if this were allowed or not. Maybe a tribe of red-backs would leap out from some innocent-looking weed. He turned his hand over; not a scratch. He smelt the earth, under the weeds, and shuddered.

The cloud was increasing, a wind rising. He thought of Susie in the caravan. He wandered back to his mother's room. 'Tread softly . . .' he read for the thousandth time. There, that was something he could do. He could look through his mum's *Collected Yeats*. See if he could find the reference. He pulled it down from a shelf and turned over the pages, reading here and there.

He supposed he should ring Simon, but not yet. Not at the moment. He didn't feel in the right mood to ring. It might spoil it, somehow. Spoil the feeling they'd had last night. He sighed, and looked for the puppy. It was curled up in its basket, sleeping the time away till Susie would come home.

He went up to his room, started going through his things. All kinds of unexpected treasures and mementoes turned up. Old tickets he'd kept from Taronga Zoo and a ride on the ferry, a picture of him with his dad. 'My two Davids', his mum had written on the back. A painting set, Susie had given him once. Probably the sort of present you give someone when you really want it for yourself. He should have given it back. He smiled as he looked at the card that was still inside it, sprawly letters in pink crayon with drawings of happy faces in every corner: 'To Davey, with all my love for a hapy bithday,' she'd written. 'And all of mine, to you,' he wrote, and put it centrally on his desk.

He was just wondering if he could face having some lunch when the phone rang.

chapter 36

HE RUSHED FOR it. Simon! It would be Simon. But it was Susie. Susie crying.

'You'll have to calm down. Tell me what's happened.'

He waited patiently, worried, for her to tell him. Susie never cried. Hardly ever. What on earth had happened? 'Sure, I'll pick you up. Just say where you'll be.' He scribbled something down on the sleeve of his T-shirt. 'Can't you give me an inkling? Okay. I'll be right there.'

It was only when she'd hung up he realised: the car. He got out the phone directory and started looking up a taxi company.

As he went to pick up the phone it rang again. Simon. He cut him short. 'Sorry, mate. Can I ring you later? Susie's in a bit of strife and I've got to get a cab. No, the car's bung. No, you definitely *can't* come round. Don't be an ass. That'd be two of us in the one car. What? What d'you mean?' But Simon had already rung off.

Maybe it was just as well, he thought, after looking in his wallet. He turned out his pockets, then searched through his mother's change drawer. He doubted he had enough to get a taxi there, let alone two ways.

He went to Susie's wardrobe and pulled out her mulberry parka. He looked out a flask, and was filling it up with hot chocolate when he heard the car. He grabbed the keys and his jacket, picked up the flask and the parka, banged the door shut, and ran down the path. The engine was running, but Simon was standing outside it, on the passenger side. 'You'll have to drive.'

David tossed him the house keys. 'In that case, you stay here. No point in us both going.'

But Simon was already levering himself in. No time to waste arguing with him. Would they get there, now, with the two of them in the car? A golden opportunity for Fate.

David revved up the street. It was a beautiful car, silver – much smoother than his mum's. He tried to talk normally, as if they were just out on any sort of outing. 'Why d'you want me to drive? Don't tell me. Three guesses. One, you've got a headache. Two, suddenly you need glasses. Three, you've been on the booze.'

'All correct,' said Simon, a bit shamefaced. 'I had a couple of glasses of wine to calm me down. What's up with Sue?'

'Don't know, but she wants to come home. I've to meet her on

South Road. Up Morphett Vale way. Some deli or other.'

'She'll be okay there, then. Take it easy, Dave.'

The sky had been getting progressively blacker, and now it began to rain. David searched for the wipers. They started at full pelt, and he had to calm them down a bit, drop them a notch on the wheel. Wet dust smeared the windscreen.

He followed Goodwood Road right down to South Road and soared up it to the steep, winding stretch with bare paddocks on either side. The car skidded slightly on a sharp bend, and, as it did so, he noticed Simon was holding on to the handle of the door. He forced himself to slow down. 'What were you saying on the phone? About Fate?'

'I was thinking maybe it's best confronted. That we should get out and confront it, instead of skulking away at home.'

'You mean we could see it as a kind of dare?'

'Something like that.'

A dare to end all dares – or them.

Motorists were starting to put on their lights, the reflections flashing up at them from the wet road. He listened to the periodic roaring and swishing of the cars. Simon had fallen silent.

'Confront your fate.' His hands had a tremor in them.

The weather had certainly broken. The rain was coming in gusts, lashing down on them. It was getting so hard to see. The squalls buffeted the car, sheeting sideways across it. In the intervals between them he could see the greying fields, the other struggling cars. The windows were steaming up. If something were going to happen, it would happen now. A tingling sensation went over him, followed by a cold wave of fear. Yet he tried to hurry, in the quiet spells at least, thinking of Susie, miserable, upset, waiting for them in some seedy deli.

But they reached it okay. And there she'd been: outside it, waiting for them. White as a sheet. Propped up against the wet weatherboard, a long stick of liquorice in her hand. She was chewing steadily, soaked through. He parked the car close in to the kerb and jumped out. 'You stay here,' he called to Simon. He ran towards her. She smelt of the sea, her hands in blue and pink patches from the cold. She didn't get up; just fished something out of her pocket. 'Thought you'd be interested in this.'

It was a photograph she handed him. A photograph of Andrea.

'Where'd you get that?'

'Greg showed it to me.'

'*Greg* was there?'

'He turned up this morning. I'd gone down early to the beach. He must have followed me. He wanted to get all pally . . .'

Susie started to shake – and she seemed to be out of breath. 'Tell me after.' He put his arm around her and opened the back door of the car. 'Take your top off and put that parka on. We won't look. I'll drive round into the side street. There's a rug there, on the floor. And a flask of hot chocolate.'

'All mod cons.' Susie tried to laugh, but there was a sob in her voice.

'Two knights . . .' said Simon, turning to grin at her.

'In white and yellow T-shirts,' she completed. 'A sort of dim shining.' She wrapped the rug around her and opened up the flask. Warm, soothing smells filled the car.

But David was feeling slightly sick. What was *Greg* doing with a photograph of Andrea? He didn't even have one himself. He stuck it in the pocket of his jeans. 'Say we get in the back with you – one each side – and you tell us all about it?' They squeezed up together. 'Now, Greg tried to get too friendly . . .'

David could see Simon flinch.

'I just walked off, round by the rocks.'

'What happened?'

'Nothing at first. Then he ran after me. He came up close, stood over me, and tried to kiss me again. When I wouldn't, he looked as if he was going to hit me instead. "You wouldn't dare," I said.

'"Oh, wouldn't I? Did you get a look at Andrea that night?"

'"You?" I said. "Andrea? You don't even *know* Andrea."'

David felt his knees turn to water.

'He said something like, Andrea was supposed to be his girl. She *was* his girl. Till she started acting stupid – "falling for your pathetic brother, showing him things."

'"Showing him things"? I asked.

'"Showing him things she shouldn't've."

'"You're making it up," I said. But then he took out this photograph . . .'

Andrea and *Greg*? David couldn't take it in.

'Then he said we weren't there to talk about Andrea, but about him and me. He sneered down at me. "Not really to talk. It's something else I have in mind. You've been giving me the run around."

'That's when I wondered if it was partly my fault. I did think once, he was kind of attractive.'

Simon winced.

'I'd started walking again, but he slapped me up against this cliff. It was jagged – it hurt me. He pinned me against it, held me with his hips, then he started yanking up my shirt . . .'

David felt a hot surge of rage followed by that tingling sensation again, all over his body. Greg, messing with Andrea, messing with his *sister*, for Christ's sake. Yet in among it all, a crumb of content: 'falling for your brother'.

He could see Simon's fists were clenched.

'I managed to twist away and run back to the caravan. But Cynth wouldn't believe me. It was horrible: she must have known it was true, just looking at me. So I made off up South Road, and rang you.'

David forced himself to get out and move into the driver's seat. Simon stayed with Susie. He revved up the car and moved out onto the busy South Road, looking for somewhere safe to turn. He felt something sharp dig into his thigh. The photograph. It was because he was still half thinking about it that he pulled off the road a little and joined a long line of cars. The back of their car stuck out awkwardly into the road.

'What you doing, Dave? We don't need petrol.'

Susie laughed, sounding more like herself. 'Don't worry. He's on automatic. He just can't resist it when it's cheap.'

'Oh.' Simon laughed too, but a bit high, not his usual laugh.

David knew that Simon would feel uneasy, vulnerable, with the bottom of the car sticking out. What a fool he was! Stopping for petrol on such a day. Tempting Fate. Cars swished by.

But nothing happened. It was okay.

'I hate to tell you,' Susie said as they drove off again, 'but there was broken glass on the road. There.' She looked back. 'Just where we were coming out.'

David groaned. 'That's all we need.' But it wasn't then, they'd got their flat tyre. He reduced his speed, just in case, but the car purred on, perfectly normally.

Susie had curled up on the seat and was looking out the back window as she had when she was small. Looking out at car lights falling into puddles. David turned the car around at an island, and headed back for O'Halloran Hill. The car cruised on.

And then he heard Susie's voice, low, husky, *rushed*. 'Hard left. Get off the road!'

David swung the wheel over and the car lurched sideways then crunched up onto the verge, over the pebbles, over the rocks that were half concealed in the long grass. A white four-wheel drive rocketed past them.

David turned round. Susie had sunk back on the seat. 'It was coming at us, Dave. I swear it was. I saw its headlights almost on us, and it wasn't slowing down. Maybe its brakes failed.'

The boys looked at one another. 'And maybe they didn't,' said Simon. 'A *white* four-wheel drive.'

David knew what Simon was thinking. All the officials' cars, lined up so neatly in The House of Records' car park, had been white. There had been two or three four-wheel drives amongst them. It made him think of something in the article Andrea had shown him. Something about due dates, the accuracy in prediction of. Something about ruling out one explanation as being too sinister . . . . But the car seemed to be listing. He reached for his jacket and got out to have a look.

The rear inner tyre had gone completely flat. The sky was so dark David knew it couldn't hold the next lot of rain much longer, but 'Susie, you'll have to get out. Sorry.'

They helped him push the car further off the road, but the verge was narrow. A small part of the car was still out on the bitumen, at an angle. *Any* part out was dangerous. David opened the boot and looked for the jack. 'Where d'you keep it?'

Simon peered in. 'Damn! Dad took it out to fix his tyre last week. He hasn't put it back.'

'There's a garage, just over there,' said Susie. 'I'll nip across and borrow one.'

'No you won't. Stay here with Simon. *I'll* go.'

He ran across the road, narrowly avoiding two or three cars. He stood fuming, almost shaking with frustration as the attendant took money for petrol, chatted to someone about the price of exhausts. He waited until he couldn't, any more. 'Please. My car. Over there.' He pointed. Susie and Simon were still on the verge. Simon had his arm around her. They both seemed to be eating on the same strand of liquorice. Maybe he should order a taxi for Susie – Simon was sure to have money or a card – but then it might be quicker just to fix up the tyre.

As the attendant went into the workshop to get him a jack, it started to pour. Sheets of water slanted across the road. There was no sign of Simon or Susie. They must have got inside. And then he thought he could see them, blond heads close together, in the front seat. Susie would be turning on the radio. But her hair wouldn't be blond, he thought. It was too wet for that.

He waited, in a fever to get back across the busy road. The attendant was coming now, a grey-blue jack in his hand. He paused to talk to someone by the pump. The pumps were white and blue, he remembered afterwards.

David watched him, wondering if he should go up and snatch the jack out of his hand. His imagination had gone haywire.

179

Through the downpour he thought he could hear the terrifying sound of screeching, of sliding, of power out of control. Then the monstrous bang of metal on metal, echoing for miles and shaking the glass windows in the closed-in area of the service station.

He grabbed the jack and, beside himself, ran across the four-lane highway, waving it. 'I'm coming! I've got it!' he yelled. Cars screeched around him. He'd made it to the island in the middle of the road and could see their car. It was all right. It was still there. But his imagination was off again. As he looked at it, he seemed to see it burst into one tall flame. He stood on the island, staring at it. The black sky, the yellow stubble field behind it, the red and yellow flames. The colours were . . . He ran towards it, towards the hot high flare. He felt as if someone were holding him back, as if he were struggling, trying to wrench himself free. Soon there would be a huge explosion; bits of metal would fly up all around him in the air. And like in the trenches, bits of . . .

But it wasn't so. The car was still there, untouched. Nothing had happened. It was all okay. His breath came in dry, hurtful, *bruising* pants. Simon and Susie were staring out at him. Out through the glass.

chapter 37

THEY WERE STARING out at him in a concerned way. 'You looked demented as you ran across the road,' said Simon. 'You still look demented. What's wrong?'

David was struggling to get his breath back. 'I got panicky. Imagined something had happened.'

'Well, it hasn't,' said Simon calmingly. 'We've eaten a bit of liquorice and got a little wet, that's all. We might even just have avoided . . .' He looked meaningfully at David. 'Here, you go with Susie, through the fence. Sit under a tree and watch me fix the wheel.'

And David let him. He'd got himself into such a state: he'd need to calm down before he could drive them home. He lifted the fence wires for Susie.

'No wonder you feel panicky,' she said. 'Anyone'd feel panicky after that car nearly hit us. My heart's *still* racing.'

The best tree they could find looked as if it had been hit on the head as an infant: a small stringy bark, and the wind still whistled through it. But it would have whistled through any tree, it was so strong now. The flags at the service station across the road were turning themselves inside out, and the cars had a sway to them as they surged, in a continuous line past them, up the South Road. They waited, under the tree. Beside him, he could feel Susie shiver. He wished he'd got her a taxi when he'd first thought of it. He'd been thinking, stupidly, that Susie being with them made it safe. But it could mean she'd be hurt. If the four-wheel drive had hit them . . . And anxiety might bring something on. Just like you feel vulnerable on Friday the 13th. Vulnerable and clumsy. There were always more accidents then, even though fewer cars were on the road. People thinking it was their destiny. Today was like that, a million times over.

Maybe it wasn't too late. 'Say I get you a taxi. You're frozen. It's no good you hanging around in this gale.'

'I'm enjoying it,' she said. 'A taxi? Don't be ridiculous. What would I do with a taxi?'

'Actually, it wouldn't be a bad idea,' said Simon, as he crawled through the fence towards them. 'The spare tyre isn't up to much.'

David stood up. 'That settles it. I'll just run across the road . . .'

'No you won't,' said Susie, her words getting partly swallowed up in the wind. 'And we've seen you "just" run across the road. There's no way I'm going home on my own.'

Simon looked at her, then at David and shrugged. 'I think we should keep off the main road. It'd be better if we went home a quieter way, where we can take it easy.'

'Good idea.' David had had enough of South Road. 'I'll turn left at Majors. It'll be a bit longer, but . . .'

'Does that take us down by Brighton?' asked Susie.

'Could do.'

'Let's stop and have some fish and chips at the kiosk. *Please*. I'm starved, and the sea'd be great, today.'

David felt uneasy, but only for a moment. Brighton was one of his 'safe' places. With infinite care he swung the car back into the traffic, and headed, as slowly as he dared, for Majors Road. The wind tore at the car as they drove along it, flat, stubbly fields on either side. But it was sheltered compared with the intersection at Lonsdale Road. They turned right, into the part of it called Ocean Boulevard, and felt the full force of the wind for the first time.

'You can smell the sea from here,' said Susie, 'even with the windows up.'

David had to keep both hands firmly on the wheel to prevent the car from being rocked from side to side. For all that, he felt much safer, more comfortable, now that they were on the sea road. Even, he felt a rising sense of elation: perhaps *that* had been meant to be their fate – back there on O'Halloran Hill – as Simon had suggested.

They ate far too many chips with their fish, and then had two tall cups of coffee each. Their table and chairs, designed for the summer, were painted white. Now that they were pleasantly full they gave proper attention to the view in their window.

The sea was broken up for miles, huge murky breakers, white-tipped, rolling in almost to the sea-wall. All around the jetty the water looked swollen. Then it would break, slap up against the thick wooden supports, send spray spectacularly over the rail and onto the timbered deck.

'It looks . . . better than anything,' said Susie. 'Like a picture, or a movie set.'

The beach was deserted: no one in sight at all, but a few sea-gulls were still battling it out with the wind.

'Let's walk out on the jetty,' said Susie.

The boys looked at her.

'Oh, I know we'll get wet, but it'll be a *bracing* sort of a wet. And we're soaked already; a bit more won't matter. It'll clear your head, Simon. You're looking all bleary.'

'I don't know,' said David. 'I think I should get you both home.'

But Simon was already getting up. 'It's good on a rough day, out on the jetty.'

David stayed behind to pay the shopkeeper. Simon had given him $20.

'Not many out today.'

'No. There should be, though. Looks great on a day like this, doesn't it?'

'*I* like it. But it doesn't bring in much cash.'

David ran out of the shop, thinking he might still be able to get Susie and Simon into the car, but when he crossed the road he could see they were already out on the jetty. It was long and straight, like a corridor. He shivered a little, and hurried after them.

chapter 38

IT WAS DIFFERENT being out here, David thought. Looking out at it through the window, you believed you were experiencing it, but the feeling of it was nowhere near the same. It was like the difference between TV and real life. It was the noise you noticed most: a wild roaring in the waves, a lost moaning in the wind. They were getting drenched, but, the more it happened, the more pleased Susie seemed to be. She was prancing around near the end of the jetty. Anyone watching them all would think they were under five.

But of course there was no one, watching.

The sea smelt strong and raw and looked angry – *black-backed* – further out, still a swollen and sullen green near the jetty. The sky was becoming darker by the minute – a threatening, ugly, thick dark grey. Rain misted the distant hills. David felt as if they were miles out from shore, cut off, in a separate world. He could see the white of the kiosk in the distance, but it could have been in another life they'd sat down to have chips at the white painted table. The shopkeeper had looked like a seaman, with a mass of dark hair and an overgrown black beard, his face lined, brown, good-natured.

Simon and Susie were still forcing their way out against the wind. David followed after them, then stopped, looked over the rail at the curving line of the beach. Dirty brown-white froth rolled across it. He stared down, into the water. It was cloudy, seething, anonymous.

He turned his head, and the wind roared in his ears. He pushed his way up the jetty, suddenly desperate to reach them. It was then, under the noise of the wind and the waves that he heard the sound. A creaking, swaying sort of a sound, almost friendly at first. *Does it always creak, the jetty?* The creaking of worn timbers. He stopped again; listened. But today it was more than a creak. The noise was growing, spreading, multiplying, even as he stood there. He held his breath. Suddenly the noise of the timbers was almost rivalling the sound of the storm. You couldn't have called it any sort of a creaking now. The sound he heard was of *cracking*. He listened again, head bent. Then tried to run, waving his arms above his head. 'Susie!' he called. 'Simon! It's going! The jetty! It's going to go!' But his words blew back in the wind.

He stopped, when he'd nearly got to them, looked around him in disbelief. The timbers near the shore end were starting to give. He could hear a wrenching, tearing noise as the sea shook the old boards, worried them, then tossed them end first into the sea. He moved on, slowly, carefully now, over the shifting boards. His ears ached in the wind.

'Hell,' said Simon.

'My dumb idea.' (Susie.)

Terrified they looked back towards the shore. Who would have thought the jetty would go?

'And at the shore end,' said David, 'and not out to sea.'

The hole was almost in line with the shore. The part over the sand was still there, but then the gap appeared over what would normally be the shallows. The two-thirds beyond it was holding – even the shelter shed at the end of the jetty was still there – but most of the planks were lumpy, were buckling up.

They huddled together.

'We'll stay here. Attract someone's attention,' said David.

They stared at the empty beach. There weren't even any cars in sight. Or only their own, waiting, silver, outside the deli.

'And the light's so bad.' (Susie.)

Simon grabbed David's shoulder. 'How long can we wait? If the rest of the jetty goes we won't even have a chance.'

It was Simon's words that made David realise: all they had *now* was a chance. And what sort of a chance was it? It was their due date: his and Simon's. At least Susie would survive. He clutched the thought to him like a flame, like a candle. But what was it Andrea had said? *Fate I don't know about. Maybe it's worth fighting against. Anyway, what would you have to lose?*

He looked around him. 'If only we had a rope.'

'I'm the lightest,' said Susie, close to his ear. 'I'll go back, very carefully, see how far we can *walk* back. Maybe we could manage two or three strokes – there, between each support where the jetty's down.'

She'd already gone. There was no point in rushing after her, to make it more dangerous. When she got near the gap in the jetty she lay flat on the timbers, edged herself in nearer.

They watched her come back. The wind bit through their T-shirts.

Susie's face was white. 'It's pretty bad. More of a hole than I thought. No chance of jumping it, especially in this wind. But one good thing, the rails are still hanging on. They're hanging down

185

in the water. We might be able to use them to get to the steps.'
She paused, to get her breath. 'I'm strongest in the water, Dave's
second. I think we should go together, try it out, then I'll come
back for you, Simon.'

'No,' he said. '*I'll* go first. It's my turn.'

David felt suddenly irritated. 'Let's not all start playing the
hero. Susie's right. If we get across, then I can run for help while
Susie waits on the beach, keeping an eye on you.'

Before Simon could argue, David wrenched off his shoes and
jacket, then, heart racing, followed Susie to the gash in the
boards. The sea was leaping up through it: released, expanding,
free.

I *can't*, he thought.

'Now, lower yourself down, Davey. That swinging handrail
should take your weight.'

'If it doesn't?'

'Swim for the next support. You'd only have to do it twice. I'll
be right behind you.'

Without looking at the water he slithered down the post and
wrapped his legs around it. The sea tugged and spat at him. So
cold. Already he was losing the feeling in his legs. He tried to grab
the rail, but it was swinging just out of reach. He looked over at
Susie, half thought of trying to climb back up. But she kept pointing to the rail. As the sea swung it towards him he lunged for it.
Missed, but now he knew what to do. He waited for it to come
towards him again, angling himself out wider. Launched himself.
There, he'd got it. But his whole body shook.

The rail was holding. He tried to move his legs, partly swimming. A wave took him, nearly knocked the rail out of his hands.
He swallowed water, but he hung on. Then reached out one arm.
Miraculously, he'd made it to the first support. He let the rail
swing back for Susie. Above him, he could hear wind and waves
tear at the loosening planks.

In a panic he swam for the steps; the sea was pulling him down.
He was running out of air, suffocating in the grey murky water, his

186

lungs bursting. What was it Andrea had said? A cross wave edged him in nearer – in his mouth the bitter taste of the sea – and he reached out for the second support. Looked back. There was Susie at the first post, *waving* to him, for Christ's sake.

Resting, filling up with air, then swinging his body round the wooden post and towards the steps. Foot on the metal step, but afraid to let go. Twisting himself round further, one *hand* on a metal step. He rested, felt the sea tear at him, but stayed firm, freezing feet and both hands hanging on. Then slowly stumbled upwards, laid himself full length on the planks. *Shaking*.

'Whew!' gasped Susie, dripping ocean, lying flat beside him.

Simon was waving to them, was making great victory signs in the air. David waved back. 'Susie, *up*! We've got to make it to the beach.'

'You go. The jetty's buckling some more. Just listen to the racket.' Her voice came out as a wail. 'I can't leave Simon alone out there. I promised.'

'He'll be okay till we get a rope.' She couldn't be such an idiot. 'It's only sense.'

He started inching his way, on hands and knees. 'Susie?'

But she wasn't listening. She wasn't coming with him. Rage engulfed him. She's choosing *Simon*, he thought. He stood up, his legs barely able to hold him. Susie, already in the water, was yelling at him, and pointing. Pointing towards the sea end of the jetty. David looked along it. The jetty was empty. Grey sea and sky and no dark figure there. He knew what it was: Simon didn't want to risk Susie coming back for him. He was going it alone. The fool!

Now Susie was hanging onto one support, Simon to another. The broken railing floated between them. David could see she was pointing at it, trying to get Simon to let go, to lunge for it as they had done. Only his face, white as death, showed out of the shifting water.

Susie was swimming in nearer to Simon, but David could see her strokes slacken, get smaller. It reminded him of that horrible race. She was struggling, *fighting* to keep her head up. 'Susie! Susie!' Simon was calling. It was the shape of the word he could distinguish, not its sound. He watched, mesmerised, as Simon let go of his support: with frail, half-movements tried to reach her. But the waves were pulling him back, or sideways.

The sea frothed and foamed around them, then hung sullen, in giant, swollen folds of ugly green. David could hear a seagull, scream overhead as he too flung himself into the sea.

chapter 39

LONG CORRIDORS WERE his now, peopled by white, wraithlike figures that came and went. Over him anonymous voices rose and fell. Sometimes a darker shape that he thought he knew was there as well: his mother, often; once, even his father; and a tall shape he thought might be Andrea. But Susie didn't come. Simon didn't come. When a shape he knew, but not theirs, hung over him, demanding of him, he turned away; turned with his face to the wall. Waited for it to go away. It was only anonymous voices he could bear now. Anonymous faces.

He had recognised the face that loomed over his on the sand, momentarily, before he went out to it again. Not Susie's. Not Simon's. A seafaring face; tanned, lined. A face with an overgrown beard.

Susie hadn't drowned, he knew that. Had been told that near the beginning. Susie had died of a heart attack. *I must be so unfit*, she'd said. Better or worse? (Either way, she'd left him.) Better, his teacher had thought. His English teacher, Mr Easterby. For later, the letters had come. He'd quoted from Hopkins, wrote: 'I found this line in your favourite poet and thought it might bring comfort. *The sea took pity; it interposed with doom.*'

He hardly knew what it meant, what his teacher wanted it to mean, to him. The worst was waking in the night, forgetting at first, only to have it come rushing back tenfold. *I wake and feel the fell of dark, not day.* Or, *My cries heave, herds-long.* These were the lines he understood.

That time passed he knew from the changing flowers that sat around him in vases. Otherwise he wouldn't have known. All days grey-white, seamless. Bandage days.

He woke once into bright light to find someone small and dark sitting beside his bed. Someone he felt he should know. Someone who, literally, had seemed part of the furniture once. He put in that room, that furniture around him. Red chair, black desk, view of the hospital roofs and further out, the city. Jim. Simon's friend. Friend of sick children and friend of those who survived. He stared at him, steadily. Brown eyes looked back.

'There's not much one can say. All clichés. And being there, seeing it all. It'll never leave you. Why pretend? But you're young. Your whole life . . .'

There was something he wanted to ask. Maybe Jim was the only one who could tell him. Something he had to know. He licked his lips. Swallowed a few times. It was a long time since he'd spoken. 'Simon.' His voice was low and cracked. 'Would he have been okay?'

Jim hesitated, perhaps only wanting to tell him what he thought he would want to hear. He could almost feel Jim turning over his answers. 'If I tell him he was better, would that make it worse? If he was going to die anyway . . .' But he saw Jim settle for the truth. 'He seemed to be okay,' he said at last. 'And he was young, strong, with a very good fighting spirit. But who knows? Nobody could say for sure. Certainly not in the longer term.'

Jim was talking about his mum, about his dad. About how strong they had been, but how they needed him now to get better. He let it all wash over him. 'And the girl. A girl came to see me. Tall, striking-looking. Anxious about you. Wondering what we did, afterwards. For the brothers and sisters. I can't think what she was called. "Anna"? "Angela"?'

And that was when David spoke for the second time. 'Andrea,' he said.

Jim was looking at the photograph he had by his bed: the photograph at the jetty, not of a funeral, his mother had insisted, but of a celebration. The minister had said it was a celebration no different from others, for *all* celebrations come after. This gathering was to celebrate two lives, now completed.

'It was early in the day,' Jim was saying. 'They came from everywhere, in cars, on bikes, on foot, all of them with flowers.' He paused. 'It was the silence you noticed most, and the smell, the smell of those lovely flowers.'

He looked at the photograph again. 'There were hundreds on the beach, clustered around the jetty. I've never seen so many young people at a funeral. And the flowers – there were *mountains* of flowers, piled up, on the sand.'

He paused again, and looked at David. 'Ceremonies like this have a healing power. Did your mother tell you about the balloons?'

David shook his head.

'There were those who found it a bizarre touch, but I found it . . . extravagant, wonderful. Some of the young people had brought balloons, *hundreds* of them. They let them off at the shore end of the jetty.'

David could imagine it all: the masses of people, the mountains of flowers, the floating balloons. 'What colour were they?'

The balloons, pulled backwards over the sea then rising up, escaping into light and space.

Jim thought back. 'Pink,' he said. 'Pink and . . . yellow. Glorious.'

'I have to go over to Simon's.'

There was a smell of Susie in the room. It was the loquat blossom. His mum had put a sprig of it on the table, the way Susie had always done. 'Does it smell of marzipan or what?' she would ask. 'I can never work it out.' He lifted it up, put it to his face. *Mountains of flowers.*

190

His mother looked at him, worried, gaunt. 'If it's what you want. Perhaps we should both get out of the house, with all this hammering going on.'

David had visited a carpenter the morning after they'd got the puppy. Paid him in advance to put a fence up. Something else he'd tried to organise, tried to order. Like seeing his dad. He'd forgotten all about it, the fence, until the hammering that afternoon. Goffie, bigger now, less soft-toyish and more dog-like, was crouched under the dining-room table letting out feeble barks.

'Maybe I'd better stay with him,' said his mum. 'Or take him for a walk. He's getting upset.'

David rode off on his bike. It wasn't that he particularly wanted to speak to Simon's mother he was going, although perhaps he owed her that much. He thought of how happy she had been the day she'd followed him up to Simon's room, her arms full of quinces. There was something he had to find out.

He hadn't rung first. Just turned up. Pushed on the bell, stood silent as the door slowly opened. 'David,' said Simon's mum, in a voice that suggested surprise, even shock. As if he had been a ghost.

She stepped aside, ushered him into the hallway. He headed down to the kitchen: dark wood table, dark cork floor. He leaned his hands on the table and looked across it at her. 'I was wondering if you'd mind if I had a look in Simon's room.'

Su-sie! Si-mon!

She looked with dull eyes into his. Her voice was flat, monotone. 'You left something there, did you? Of course, go on up. Nothing's touched.'

He climbed the stairs he had run up so light-heartedly that last time. Susie had been waiting in the car with Peaches. There had been a message for him on the screen saver. 'Back at twelve', it had said. He'd wondered, as he lay there in hospital, if Simon might have left him one last message, just in case, just on the off-chance. He'd been going to leave letters for everyone else. He turned on the computer, clicked on 'apple' and then on the control panel. It filled the screen. On the *After Dark* programme he highlighted 'messages'. He stuck in a disk at random. It turned out to be Simon's latest history essay, 'due 18 June'. He'd highlighted the date and given it a string of exclamation marks.

A minute or so went by. Then the screen went black and the message started to come. It was a scrolled message, emerging from the right of the screen and moving steadily left. The first word was coming across, in capital letters on a 24 point size. 'EXPERIMENT', it said slowly, and then, in a smaller point, in ordinary letters: 'one healthy, one sick' and then, 'EXPERIMENT'. David watched the message repeat itself, over and over again. It shifted down the screen and then came in again higher up, but always the same message, over and over. He watched as the letters formed, then disappeared and re-formed. 'EXPERIMENT'. The word sank into his mind. He remembered now: that had been the ten-letter word placed centrally (and illegally) on the Scrabble board the day Andrea had come to tea. It had been Simon's word.

But now a second message was coming across: 'GUY – hospital'. The words scrolled their way across the space of the screen.

What Simon wouldn't tell him; hadn't told him until now. 'Who is this guy?' he'd asked, over and over, almost shaking him once. But Simon said he'd promised not to tell. This 'guy' had told Simon the surveillance system was switched off. He remembered how they'd squatted, absurdly, on the shut toilet seats, while the camera hung placid on the wall.

But there was more to it than that. This guy had told Simon to take someone with him. Had he a friend, a girlfriend, perhaps, who would go with him? *'Maybe a girl would be better. Has this David got a sister? It doesn't need to be a girlfriend.'*

The last time he'd been in here, he'd seen something in Simon's journal – a little red book. It had been open at a page. David hadn't really meant to read it, but his eyes had just, accidentally almost, floated over it. *Why did he want me to take Susie?*

So. It had been Susie the whole time, not him at all. 'One

healthy, one sick,' said the message. Except Susie had been sick too, without their knowing. He remembered how she had lost the unlosable race at the pool. 'I got so out of breath,' she'd said. And later, after the car had nearly hit them, gasping, under a tree.

It would have been 'this guy' who'd suggested to Simon in the first place that he find out about his due date. Maybe Simon had been baulking at the treatment. Or some of it. Yes, that would have been what it was. Simon had mentioned it in the car once, on the way to Middleton, it'd been. 'At least I got out of the chemo.' A prime subject for experimentation. 'Find out, then,' the doctor would have said, 'and then we'll know how to proceed. Or whether we should proceed at all.'

He thought back to that last attempt, the 'successful' attempt at The House of Records, the abseilers swinging outside. That thug Greg swinging outside. It hadn't been 'successful' in that sense at all; it was the authorities who had been successful. 'Let them see the records, but let it appear to be of their own volition, their own choice.' Otherwise of course, your anger would target the authorities, and not your fate. And that wouldn't be the kind of experiment they wanted.

He remembered Simon's phrase: 'outside permission'. He'd meant that they'd done what was not allowed. Now the phrase took on a more sinister aspect. Permission from the outside.

He tried to think back to that night. He had used his small, personal torch. It had been flickering. Maybe his eye had slipped a line. Read Susie's date, and not his own. Or had they shifted the lines, knowing it was David and not Susie who would come?

Perhaps Simon had worked it out. He sifted through the mound of papers by his window, the window that looked out onto the kidney-shaped pool. Darkening poplar leaves lay thick across it, a twig trying to float through these drifts of silent leaves. Along the veins they turned brown first, then writhed upward, drying, crackling, before going flaccid and black. Simon had talked about leaves; but not leaves like these. His dead leaves, defying the cars, had seemed *triumphant*.

193

What was it Jim had said? 'There's no use being angry, David. It's just something that happened. No one knows why. It happens to everyone, and it happened to him early, that's all.'

'That's all!' he'd screamed, thinking of the autumns Simon, Susie would never see, thinking of the swimming pool filling up with dead leaves. Mounds of them, piling up high. *Though worlds of wanwood leafmeal lie.* But it wasn't like that: not pretty, like the Hopkins image.

And on the jetty, he'd been *irritated* with Simon. 'I'll go first,' Simon had said. And then something else: something about his 'turn'. 'It's my turn.' As if they were playing some sort of a game – or waiting in a queue at the end of some long corridor. And he'd been *angry*. 'Let's not all start playing the hero . . .' The last words he'd said to his friend.

The journal wasn't by the window. He started looking through the drawers of the desk, on the floor beneath it, behind the computer, even under Simon's pillow. No sign, anywhere. He couldn't rummage further than that, although the wardrobe lay open, and it might just be in a pocket. His clothes hung in silent rows, like Susie's. He could see the shape of Simon's knees in the jeans he must have worn the day or so before it happened.

He shut the wardrobe door and looked over at the computer. 'GUY – hospital' was still scrolling its way across the screen. He would have liked to change its message, as he had that last time. He turned back to the control panel, to 'edit message' on the *After Dark* programme. He tried *The sea took pity . . .* , but that didn't seem right. He stared at the letters, so black on the white screen. Into his mind came a line of Yeats he had read on Susie's, on Simon's, last day:

All that's beautiful drifts away
Like the waters.

That would do for his first message. Something else, then, for the second. He dropped his head over the keys. He knew what he would've liked to put: the text of the minister's address. *And death shall have no dominion.*

194

His mother had said to him, later, when he'd come home, 'I wish you could have been there. Everyone who was, will remember it. Always. There was such a sense of peace.'

David saw it all again: the sea, the flowers, the masses of people. Perhaps you could look at the words of the text not in a divine but in a human sense: Susie, Simon, living on in the memory of everyone who cared about them. The past running along beside you, as a writer had put it once on TV. And thinking of that meaning, his fingers reached for the keys.

He clicked back to Simon's essay and waited till first one message and then the other, scrolled its way across the screen. He turned the computer off and ran down the stairs.

He would have kept running, run straight home, but Simon's mother called out to him from the kitchen. 'Freshly brewed coffee and almond biscuits.' She must have seen the flight in his face, for she added, pleaded even, 'Do stay.'

She'd put the coffee, the biscuits and the two small brown coffee cups and saucers onto a tray, and was taking it through to the main sitting room. It was the room with the bay window, the room that looked out onto the majestic part of the garden: the expansive lawn, the huge gums, ending in the massive stone wall. He'd seen a garden that was a miniature of this. He sat, uneasily in the window alcove, the light streaming in far brighter than in the kitchen, brighter at this time of the day than in Simon's room. She pulled over a table, highly polished. The room was immaculate, beautifully and expensively furnished, the carpet pale, of powder blue.

He looked out of one side of the bay window, wishing they were in the kitchen. He felt exposed here, over-bright, the room nightmarish in its perfection. It was a room that held no trace of Simon. He lifted his cup, relishing its rich steam almost without thinking, and then felt ashamed that he could extract comfort from such small things, even now. He bolted a couple of biscuits. It made you feel real, to eat.

He would have to break the silence. 'I was wondering about Simon's journal. With the red cover?'

195

'Oh yes.' She was stirring at her coffee, endlessly. 'The journal the hospital wanted him to keep.'

'The hospital.' His voice was flat. Simon's clothes had come out of the hospital in a brown paper bag. The quinces had been in a paper bag too.

'Yes. They thought it would help when he was so sick. Keep a record. Watch yourself get better, that kind of thing.'

'I'd like to read it. Simon wouldn't have minded, I know he wouldn't.' He was talking faster, almost excited.

'You'd be welcome, David, of course. But unfortunately it isn't here. A doctor from the hospital came to collect it very soon afterwards. I was surprised, actually, at how soon it was. He said it helped them to help others. In the same situation. I was sorry when I thought about it later. I should have said I wanted to read it first.'

'GUY – hospital.' He *bet* he'd come soon afterwards. Indecently soon. Running, all the way, out of his damn hospital.

'Maybe we could get it back.'

'Perhaps. But I'm not even sure what his name was. He seemed to take it for granted that I would know. "I was Simon's doctor," he said, as if I should know him. But there were so many doctors. I didn't like to ask.'

The biscuits were nearly finished now. David ate steadily on. He'd had two cups of coffee and was starting on his third. He could see she was still trying to tell him something. He braced himself.

'He was lucky to have a friend like you. He'd have been so glad that *you* were all right. On the beach, you know, they thought you were . . . Living for him as well, now, in a way. You were always so close.'

David looked down, held the cup in his hands to warm them. He could do without this kind of talk. 'Living for him as well'.

'And he was fond of Susie too. Very fond.'

David waited, silent, still, but squirming somewhere far inside.

'I like to think maybe they're together, some place.'

196

That really had to be it. Enough. He put his cup back heavily on the tray and rose to his feet. He struggled to get his voice right. 'It's kind of you, Mrs Hatherley, but I have to be going. Mum will . . .'

'Of course. Of course, David. Do come again.'

The sun was dropping low in the window, was setting the lounge walls glowing in yellow and pink.

He got up shakily, meaning, if he could, to run; for ever from that room, for ever from that house, let himself out of the silent stone wall. But as he did so, he glanced at her face. It made him think of someone else who had lived behind stone walls, some-one else who had known despair.

He reached out his hand, put it over hers. 'Meg,' he said.

And suddenly all he could picture were balloons, Susie's, Simon's, rising off the sea like prayers.

About the Author

Eleanor Nilsson is one of Australia's most highly regarded writers for children. Her first novel for older readers, *The House Guest*, was winner of the 1992 Australian Children's Book of the Year Award, winner of the 1992 South Australian Festival Award for Literature (Children's Books) and winner of the 1992 Victorian Premier's Literary Award (Children's Books).

Eleanor is also known for her stories for younger readers, including *The Black Duck* which was shortlisted for the 1991 Australian Children's Book of the Year Award (Young Readers). Her first book, *Parrot Fashion*, was published in 1983, and since then she has written many stories that live long in the hearts of children everywhere, such as the ever-popular *Heffalump?* books and some delightful picture books like *Tatty*. Another of her books is *Writing for Children*, a guide for beginning writers.

Eleanor Nilsson lives in Coromandel Valley, Adelaide, with her husband Neil and has two grown-up children, Catherine and Martin.